Anguished to the Grave

Anguished to the Grave

F. L. Day

Published by Felipe Lopez
Contact: lopezdaywriter@gmail.com
First Printing, 2025.
Manuscript Updated: October 1, 2025

Paperback ISBN-13: 979-8-9923645-1-4
Hardcover ISBN-13: 979-8-9923645-2-1
Digital ISBN-13: 979-8-9923645-0-7

For My Grandmother,

Marilyn

Table of Contents

Preface

All my life, I have been told that I worry too much. Growing up, I was scared of inclement weather, particularly tornadoes. In my teenage years, I was terrified about what other people thought of me. Now in my early twenties, I have been afraid of never finding love or not being successful. While *The Hollowed Dreams* was all about perhapsing and pondering about my life goals and mortality, I strove to find another meaning in the poetry that I've written.

The truth is, I have quite a few fears, especially surrounding death. I am terrified of dying, even though I've been told that I'll "worry myself to death." I'm worried about not fulfilling what I want for my life before I meet my demise, and I've also been worried about not finding love before I die. Strange, isn't it? This has been where my priorities lie apparently.

To begin, I want to take you back to the Summer of 2024 when I was writing my first poetry book. I had accomplished so much at that moment, such as finishing a 90,000-word novel called *Death and the Groomsman*. This novel was focused on a civilization of Grim Reapers, with one of them falling in love with a mortal, something that would counter my little fear of death. I finished this novel in May, and I began re-working my first "real" work, *The Shadow in the Shallows*. Much like the previous novel, this one focused heavily on one of my other fears; the fear of living.

While I was doing this, I was on Facebook and stumbled across an ad from BookLeaf Publishing for a 21-day writing challenge. I would get the opportunity to pay fifty dollars to enter the contest and the publishing company would produce my very own poetry book. This was how my debut book, *The Hollowed Dreams* was born.

However, in the midst of creating *The Hollowed Dreams*, the thought occurred to me that if I wanted to, I could do the publishing process again, this time through Kindle Direct Publishing, making me my own boss, and producing a book that would fulfill my vision for a brand-new poetry book.

After sending off *The Hollowed Dreams* manuscript, I immediately began working on the next poetry book, and I already had a great title picked out, which followed what I called my computer. The only problem was that the name was already taken for a musical album by a band that I had never heard of, so I dabbled with the name again. I once said that anguish was my favorite pastime and I knew that portion of the title had to stay, but I couldn't figure out what to have with it.

Finally, I came up with a good title, *Grave Anguish*. It wasn't taken and it came from a poem that I had written for this poetry book. It was perfect! Except my brain took the title a step further and *Anguished to the Grave* popped into my head. I couldn't pick which one I liked better and neither could my coworkers. Finally, I picked the latter as the name of this book and then changed the poem around slightly to fit it as well.

Next came the bigger issue. I wanted this poetry book to be long, and that meant writing a ton of poems and even losing count of how many. It wasn't until October that I realized how many poems I had and that was when the book became more of a reality. It was official now; I was going to create a big poetry book!

While this was going on, several things would happen. I had challenges with my last semester of college, I had self-doubts about the book, and the 2024 elections were taking place, which meant that my depression was on the horizon. I just kept writing more and more depressing poems with some upbeat poetry making an appearance for once! Regardless, I had concocted so many poems and I wanted to do something that I had done once before when I was writing a book series back in high school. I wanted to split my book up into sections. This was when I realized that I could split up the poetry book into four sections, with around twenty-one poems in each section. I struggled to figure out what kind of topics come in fours, before stumbling across the stages of decomposition, which includes five stages.

"Fresh" took my first section. It was perfect. A fresh new poetry book was here, and it started out with a poem calling back to *The Hollowed Dreams*. The second section for "Bloat" was a perfect fit too as this is the section with the most already-written poems from earlier stages in my life. I revised them and plugged them in, thinking that this was supposed to be their fate all along! Decay typically comes in two stages: Active and Advanced Decay. I decided to combine the two into one section as "Decay." This was probably the most agonizing portion to write about. The final one was going to be "Skeletonization." This represented the fact that I was going to throw in a few surprises, all falling in place to call back to the beginning of my story.

In truth, *Anguished to the Grave* became more than just a poetry book, it actually became the story of my life during not only the eight months that it was constructed but also everything that came before it.

"Skeletonization" itself had to consist of not just poetry, but instead of my vision of where my writing was going and where I wanted to go forward. This means that *Anguished to the Grave* is actually a poetry collection with two short stories, one that merges with the universe in which my novels take place and the narrative in which I concocted my poetry books. This means that this poetry book and *The Hollowed Dreams* are now connected with its siblings and any book that I write from here on out will be connected to this narrative and to my life.

What I hope you gain from this poetry book is not that anguished feeling that threatens to tear you apart. I've been there and it sucks. I want you to read these words and feel the hope that's always present in the darkness, even when you think that all hope is lost. This comes at a time when you look at the news and see that your rights are being taken away, or you find out that your state is trying to pass a pointless bill that is only going to harm citizens instead of getting something done. I don't want you to feel hopeless, instead, I want you to keep fighting like I have to. Everyone that I care about keeps telling me that everything will be okay as long as we continue to fight for our rights, fight for the freedom that we believe in, and fight for the lives that we want to live. This is what I want you to take away from this literary collection. I want you to read these poems and short stories and feel like you've gained a voice, feel empowered, or feel like you can conquer depression. Take my words and cherish them as I have and perhaps together, we can make this world a world worth living in.

Above all, never stop fighting, never give up, and do not end up anguished to the grave. We are not dead yet, so stop planning your own funeral!

With all the love for the world and all things in it,

Felipe "Feeps" Lopez Day

Felipe Lopez Day

He Who Is **NOT**
Anguished to the Grave

7

BOOK I:
FRESH

"Goodbye Darkness"

Dearly Beloved,
We are gathered here today
To bear witness the end of
A man left to his demise.

This man lived a life filled with
Terrible anxiety and self-doubt.
Scared to live boldly and terrified
Of accidentally committing a wrongdoing.

Dearly Beloved,
We see the truth in its full light
Exposed to vast errors and inequalities.
Now, we do hope you stay for
A little while and listen close.

Now come! There's much to discuss,
Let us discuss the end of F. L. Day
And his poor fantasies,
You know them as
The Hollowed Dreams.

What is it that you already know?
Is it horror, the tragedy,
The great disruptions under the skin?
Regardless of what it is,
We lay him to rest today.

We could talk about these
Sad and miserable dreams,
How he thought he could go on,
Where he's filled with endless regret,
Loving silly city boys
That are way out of his league,
The lost and faded memories,
Where he felt stuck in place,

Where he's confronted
About being a monster,
Or when he's feeling like
He's made it so far,
Questioning his existence,
Feeling great sadness,
Fading into the darkness,
Losing his words,

Keeping track of his great
Little inventories,
Or when he's long gone,
Letting darkness overpower him,
Enjoying the sunset,
Hollowed out memories,
Or feeling apathy when he's
Stuck in the writer's room,
Embracing graduation,
Or finally calling it over.

I guess we'll never know.
This is his fate that
We're talking so much about.
F. L. Day is abrasive, you'll
Never find anything unless you're looking.

Dearly Beloved,
We are gathered here today
To bring forth a legend,
Torn apart from my dreams.
Here we get to witness the
Change from gay depression
To the darkness of gay rage.

So, grab your pencil,
And look up the potential.
My powers are engraved in stone.

For what remains was once unknown,
There's a new destiny to save,
So I won't be
Anguished to the Grave.

Join me down this path
And watch me voice my wrath.

We go down this path of
Unexpected results, and
We will see if we make it out
Alive.

"Not Dead Yet" (Extended)

Originally published in the Student Literary Journal, *Allusions*, by Indiana State University

There will be no one to hold my hand,
But I refuse to be like a dried fish in the sand.
The world around me is freezing over,
But I feel as lucky as a four-leaf clover.
I stand warmer than the sun and you cannot freeze me.

I stand firm and I holler,
But you may want me to wear a firm collar.
I will not bow down to control and instead I see
The crystal-clear world around me.
Don't say I won't amount to anything.

I will rise again like the dead,
And not meant to be filled with dread.
Although it might sound a bit cryptic,
It might also sound apocalyptic.
You forget, I am not dead yet.

My words might sound bland,
While I make a fist with my hand.
Trust is not something around me,
And it might not help that you might be too blind to see
That I am worth more than you'll ever be.

But I will never give a care in the world
About what you say about me,
For I know what is true.
Don't even think about burying me alive,
For I know my true self-worth.

I am not marked by a stone in the graveyard.
I am alive and well, holding up a card.
You do not have control over my life.
Once it is knocked out of your hand, I take the knife.
You forget that I am not dead just yet.

I will rise again like the dead,
And not meant to be filled with dread.
Although it might sound a bit cryptic,
It might also sound apocalyptic.
You forget, I am not dead yet.

No, I am not dead yet.
I will stand firm and I will continue to holler.
You might hate the way that I hold myself together,
But I will have a smile across my face.
No... I am not dead just yet.

You want me to whimper and cry,
I dealt the cards,
And that much is true.
I do not lay in the ground yet.
I am alive and well and you may hate that.

I will rise again like the dead,
And not meant to be filled with dread.
Although it might sound a bit cryptic,
It might also sound apocalyptic.
You forget, I am not dead yet.

They can drag me down,
They can light my work on fire.
They can even poke me in the ass with a broomstick,
But no one will never, never ever
Be better than me.

You can grab me by the neck,
And shout slurs to my face.
What you didn't foresee
Would be how well I hold myself together.
I will never fade into the darkness again.

For even in death,
I will always rise again,
And you won't even manage
To try to destroy me.
I am more powerful than you will ever be.

You're too late.
That poor and quiet little boy is too far gone now.
He stepped away from the darkness.
You see, he got tired of you stepping all over him,
And what remains is not dead yet.

Ha! Dare to tell me that I will just
Drop out of college when it gets tough.
I am not the quitter that you think I am,
And I will make sure you know
That you were dead wrong.

Don't you dare try to deny it.
I remember everything.
Grudges stay alive in my veins
And your words shall never die,
You can kiss my ass goodbye!

I will rise again like the dead,
And not meant to be filled with dread.
Although it might sound a bit cryptic,
It might also sound apocalyptic.
You forget, I am not dead yet.

I remember when you told me that I needed to grow up.
I had a lot of anger residing in me that just got built up.
I remember when you were drunk all the time,
While I was busy forging myself while in my prime.
I wanted to die every time that you opened your mouth.

You told me how I'd amount to nothing in life,
And how in my death, I'd be nothing but forgotten.
You said that no one will even give a care in the world
As a person rots down beneath the dirt.
You forget that we aren't dead yet.

I will rise again like the dead,
And not meant to be filled with dread.
Although it might sound a bit cryptic,
It might also sound apocalyptic.
But you just happened to forget, I am not dead yet.

Quit mourning yourself before you're even dead.
Our lives are not meant to be filled with dread.
I am not trying to be cryptic,
But you're acting like the world's being apocalyptic.
We aren't in the dirt just yet.

Love how you'd tell me that I am too young
To be stressed out, dismissing my feelings entirely.
Teaching me that my emotions would never matter
To anybody and that I should suffer in silence.
You can leave along with your toxic masculinity.

Or how you told me that I can't even get a sentence
Out of my mouth, let alone the fact that the anxiety
That caused this was partly because of your presence.
Don't try to tear me down when you know you caused it.
Oh but look at that, it looks like I can speak now, huh?

Just get out the door already. Get out.
I don't even want to see your face ever again.
Leave behind the memories and leave us alone.
Don't tell me how I will be nothing but a failure,
When you're already one yourself.

I used to tell myself about how much
Of a disappointment that I was to this family,
But I guess it takes the disappointment to keep
The dead remembered long after their stories were lost,
And how they are immortalized
By a stone in a graveyard.

I will rise again like the dead,
And not meant to be filled with dread.
Although it might sound a bit cryptic,
It might also sound apocalyptic.
You forget, I am not dead yet.

I am not just the boy who hangs out with the dead,
I am not just the boy who writes with dread,
I am the boy who has overcome oppression,
And you shall never begin to question
Whether or not if I am still alive.

So don't begin to mourn yourself,
Grow confidence in yourself.
Live every moment like it's your last,
And never take what you have for granted.
We're not dead just yet.

"Family Tragedy"

Growing pains aren't ever easy, and they may be quite queasy. In an old house that we used to call home, we would come around and happily gather, although, at times I would feel unwelcome and roam. I do miss the simple times and there's nothing I would rather see. We would bring food and smile, maybe laugh for a while. I would instead pretend to smile and maybe look at the ceiling tile. That all changed when the owner fell ill, and we went to a place where we sighed goodbye. The smiles faded, and the tears would come, all to which I would let out a cry. It all sounds sad and simple, but to us, it was all too real to be cheesy. The owner lived, but we lost the house, and years later, we would lose the owner too, and it was all up to a debate.

We lost Grandma years ago, and since we split, we all lost and soon went on to quit. Drifted apart, we are slowly becoming. Will I suffer the same fate even though I go a different way?

Searching for those who had once said goodbye to the world they had once lived. Stones placed in the soil are dated from birth to death. To learn from those who had passed, ancestors who lived lives, some who held faith, and others who held knives. My family continues to separate.

I keep learning and will never quit. Our family has encountered much challenge and pain, and though we may be going our separate ways, we will come together eventually, and our bond will not be slain.

"Marilyn"

I remember the day
You were born.
Your little body,
So innocent, wrapped in
That little pink blanket.

I held you in my arms,
Thinking about the future
For my perfect daughter.
Your brown eyes lit up
At the sight of me.

I introduced myself like
An idiot, expecting you to
Understand my shallow voice.
You closed your eyes when
You were done, not shifting,
And staying in place.

Your dad and I sang to you
Each and every single night.
You chuckled as you got older,
Criticizing our bad singing.
We'd laugh too, not caring,
But just having fun.

I remember showing you
My books, letting you
Hold them in your tiny hands.
Your face lit up with glee,

Your eyes twinkling, realizing
That your daddy was an author.
Conquer your dreams darling,
Anything is in reach,
You just have to work for it.

A hug goodbye as I left
You at your kindergarten class
Left me feeling so hollow.
Your bright brown eyes threatened
To fill with tears, even though
I told you daddy would never
Be too far away.

Don't forget when you
Were eight, learning how to
Ride your pink bike, but
You crashed into a tree,
Crying about your injury.
Don't worry, my sweet,
Daddy can fix anything.
I promise.

Filled with the memories
Of my own mother who
Had to run my world
And a grandmother who
I thought was always
Disappointed in me,
Your namesake, little Marilyn.

I remember when you were
Thirteen, mad that I took
Away your phone on my birthday,
Tears and screams ensued.
I forgot, little Miss Marilyn Day
Thinks she's gonna rule
The day today.

Your dad told me not to worry,
But I did regardless,
As I always do.
You couldn't handle the
Divorce well, and my mom
Knew you'd be upset.

When you were sixteen,
I taught you how to drive.
You did so well, learning so fast,
Like a true Day would.
That night you had your
Boyfriend over, and when I
Called you down for dinner,
I caught you both drinking.

"Why do you have to ruin
Everything, Dad!? Just let
Me live my life!"

I tried so hard to remain
Calm, but my temper ate at me.
Two weeks later, you both broke up.
Was it my fault? Was it?

Your aunt told me that
I just needed to give you
Your space, but it was hard.
I had always
Been there for you.
I tried my best.

When you were eighteen,
You went into college.
I dropped you off,
Hugged you close.
You heard my stories
About my college days in
A pandemic, and about
My horror stories.

God, don't let that
Happen to my dear.

You came home on
Weekends and I'd fix
Your favorite meal.

"Tell me a story dad."
A story? Like I used
To tell you when you
Were younger?
"I always loved hearing
About your grave hunting,
Is there anything you left out?"
Oh my God! What do I say?

Stay away, Marilyn.
The dead tell you secrets,
Secrets you can't bear to keep.
Your namesake tried, and
Then I tried.
Misery and disappointment
Await here. Don't you dare.

You didn't listen.
Like me and your
Great-grandmother, you
Hunted them down, and
You learned the hard way.

When you fell, I picked
You up and confronted
My demons. I lost.
You apologize again and again,
Thinking you let me down.

You never could.
Little Miss Marilyn Day
Was a fully grown woman today.
You had your wedding planned.
Dad and I walked you down
That beautiful aisle.

Just like I did at mine,
I saw everyone we had lost.
We woke them all up,
Everyone that came before,
Including your namesake.

They smiled at the wonderful
Young woman that you are.
You and your cousins are their
Successors. In your hearts,
They shall always remain.

Your new husband kisses you,
And there's the new happy couple.
Of course you kept the Day name.
I fought hard battles to get it.

Here she is, Miss Marilyn Day,
She'll rule the day today.
And by her side,
I will always remain.
My beautiful daughter…

P.S.

My beautiful daughter,
I wish you could exist.
America does not respect women,
And I'd hate for you to
Live in a constant state
Of the gravest anguish.
Blame those around us,
And please know that
I tried for us both.

"Hollow"

I feel so hollow
When I talk to
A cute guy.
My brain's machinations
Are thwarted by fear.

Is this my fate, to be
Locked in the closet,
With no one around me?
All the guys want is
To exploit my body,
It makes me feel so hollow.

Love's such a damn lie,
No one ever wants a life.
All I ever wanted was
A good damn life,
But my life is a damn lie.

So there's a new guy, and
I'm totally getting jealous.
Wondering what the hell
Is wrong with me?
I'm just so desperate anyway.

So, there's a new guy, and
He talks with tender sweetness,
But he wasn't ever
Loyal to me, so I
Gave up on him, moving on.

Then there's a new guy.
He's so sweet, but I
Had to end it before
Anything ever began.
This is my horrible fate.

Then there's this new guy,
His views are so hollow,
But his tender voice
Makes me so excited.
Should I run off with him?

No. I shan't, but
He is so tempting.
Stop it, brain, just stop.
Think clearly and move on,
For falling in love is just a myth.

I feel so hollow,
The guys can call me
A coward, but this coward's
Gonna run away...
To where no person
    Will ever find him.

"Anguished to the Grave"

Sure, I might be digging up
My own grave by speaking out,
But I don't care as this is my cup
Of tea. Cut my tongue out then!

Who do I think I am? No honey,
Who do you think you are?
You act like you've got all the money,
And your judgment has left me
Anguished to the Grave.

You don't get to tear people down,
And you sure as hell don't get to
Make me feel like I should drown.
Is this the consequence of being anguished?

No you don't get to make me feel down,
Life will get even eventually.
So don't act like you rule this town.
Your attitude is beneath you.

Don't tempt me for I can
Leave you anguished to the grave,
And you can't even ban my power,
Nor cut my tongue out.

"They Can't Know Anything"

I must be more careful,
They can't know anything
About me. It'll be the end.
However, they probe with
Their endless questions, but
They can't know anything.
Does this make me cruel?

Oh! But they know too much!
They're inferring things about me.
This is the end, is it not?
For this can not be the beginning.
I'm so lost with my own desolation.
They can't know anything,
Even if it means my destruction.

I'll feed them the wrong
Information, and they'll know
Nothing. I'll hide my truth,
For they can't know anything.
Ignorance will save me,

    … even if I die trying.

"My Work Outweighs the Pain"

Press the pedal to the floor,
You know how to make a thrill
The actors know their gore
From their plots to kill.

You whispered in my ear,
Of all the dirty things you'd do,
But I'm all lost in fear.
Did you think all this through?

And after we robbed the bank,
You threw our guns in the back,
My heart fluttered before it sank.
You grinned, holding the money sack.

You whispered in my ear,
Telling me that we're rich now,
There's no reason to fear
Or have a holy cow.

When we got back to HQ,
You smiled ear to ear.
The crime lord told us our queue,
But something remain rather queer.

I pointed my gun at you,
Your smile disappeared.
Before you pleaded, I shot through
Your charming face, your blood smeared

All over the carpet, and I
Walked all over you,
Before I shot the crime lord in the eye.
I can be powerful too.

Never trust a schemer,
He's gonna look right through you,
I rose up higher than a dreamer,
Not daring to say the words "I do."

There's no reason to fear now,
For only I remain.
I run out to my car and take a bow.
My work outweighs the pain.

"Downpour"

The rain outside patters
Against the pavement.
Time will only tell when
This storm will lift its
Might from my world.

I tried to feel something
In the midst of the rain.
I ran outside, bracing the
Downpour, not caring about
The consequences that awaited me.

I hoped that you'd come
Back around to greet me,
Except no one ever showed up.
The downpour continued...
The thunder struck, the drums
Breaking my heart's strings.

I fell down flat on the
Dead and cold grass.
I didn't care if sickness
Would be the only outcome,
For I only wanted to die.
You never came back for me,
And I just rotted away.

The selfish vultures tore
My body to pieces, and I
Couldn't pick myself up.
The downpour carried my
Entrails down to the river.

My sour brain was carried
Away. My heart shattered
Into a thousand pieces.

When they came to find me,
They saw the message
Written in my tears.
Anguished to the grave,
I wept in the downpour,
Hoping my prince would come
To save me.

Little did I know,
My death shouldn't have
Happened in the downpour.

The rain outside patters
Against the pavement.
Time will only tell when
This storm will lift its
Might from my world.
However, no one was able
To know. For I gathered
My insides into my cold,
Dead corpse, and I retired
To begin anew.

The downpour ended,
And so too did my trust.

"I Remember"

I remember those shocked
Smiles and those jaw dropping
Moments that passed us by.
I remember getting published
That very first time.
I remember Halloween costumes
And a beautifully made birthday cake
To which I acted like an ass.
And I remember feeling inadequate
With my wannabe dating problems,

But I also remember feeling
Happiness after bitter-sweet
Comfort after heartbreak,
I remember feeling helpless and
Powerless, but not around those
I cared most about.

I remember finding those lost
Gravestones, feeling so mystically
Empowered that it became
My entire personality.
I also remember those
Politically charging discussions.
I remember all those times
That I had to keep pushing on
Even though I felt so disgusted.

I remember coming home on
Weekends, reminded of how I
Couldn't bear another week
Here, hoping I could just
Be in my tiny town with
My tiny problems.

I remember feeling happiness
When I returned to campus,
Reunited to all the happy
Faces I thought I'd exhausted.

Dear Memories,
We had a good run,
It goes down with
A bold, setting sun.
Even though college is over,
Returning back to my
Tiny, little town,
With my tiny problems,
My life is far from over,
Far from the end of a page.

It's the end of a long,
Almost unbearable chapter.
Surviving a pandemic,
Catching Covid twice,
And making my final stand.

The future is so uncertain,
But it doesn't stop here.
Dear Memories,
I'll always remember you.

"Denial"

The news hit me like a bus.
At first, I didn't understand
Why anyone would have made a fuss.
The pressure is hard to withstand.
My mind is blank
Like a painter's untouched canvas.
Hearts had sank,
But my face hit the canvas.
My thoughts are blank.
This can't be happening.
It can't be happening.

Things were alright just yesterday,
But now...
Now...
It's all over.

To ignore the devastation I go.
Yes, ignore, ignore, ignore,
To ignore the devastation...
I fail.

My mind is filled with shock
And is in utter disarray.
I must remain strong,
They'd want me to be...
Denial, I must deny
I must deny.

"Fear Looks Good on You"

Oh honey! Fear looks good on you!
I love how you tremble in your boots as
You think you're telling someone off.
What was it that you were trying to accomplish?

Maybe you were just too busy on trying to be popular
Instead of becoming intelligent, and maybe you just
Spent too much time watching the news instead of
Learning some empathy for yourself.

Oh man! What was God thinking when he made you?
With every action you take, his face is red
From making contact with his palm.
What exactly are you?

You think you're a holy savior
While your wine glass is empty?
Who do you think you are to sit so high and mighty?
Oh honey! Fear looks good on you!

I really hope you were drunk when you decided
To move your little fingers, not expecting the outcome.
You should have thought a few steps ahead,
because it's never wise to piss off an English Major.

Oh honey! What's the matter with you?
Is your fear clouded with all that I hope for?
Oh my, that must be a sincere problem, so get
Wrecked, because fear looks so good on you.

And are you surprised that this is my reaction?
You clearly must have forgotten that
Anguish has always been, and forever will be
My greatest pastime.

"I Love That For You"

I love that for you,
The fact that your hatred
Has met hope, making your face blue.
Little by little, it eats you up.

Your condescending hatred shows,
Calling at others for no reason.
It's almost like your life blows,
And you're losing your grip.

I just love that for you,
Because karma will catch up
To you, it'll split your heart in two.
Perhaps, it was long overdue.

So don't come cryin' to me
When you're all sad and lonely.
Your hatred made you unable to see
How much you hurt us.

That's okay though, karma
Gets even eventually,
And yours will be encased as terre firma.
I just love that for you.

I just love that for you,
As the consequences catch up to you,
And your face turns blue.
I just love that for you!

"Does Guilt Possess You?"

We hooked up in your
Room last summer
While I concocted my manuscript.
You look at me in class,
Pretending to not even know me.

I was careful, like you wanted.
I didn't dare tell my friends,
And kept my mouth shut
To the entire world.
Does guilt possess you?

You drape your arms around
Your blond girlfriend,
Where she fails to know
The truth about you and me.
Does guilt possess you?

I tried to call your number,
But you let me go to
Your voice mail. Ignorance
Will never be bliss.
Does guilt possess you?

Would your Republican
Parents look down on you?
Would your girlfriend leave you?
Could they handle the fact that
You did unholy things to me?

You told me that you've never
Felt this complete with anyone.
You feared your parents would
Disown you for being bi, so
Does the guilt eat at you?

When I tried to talk to you,
Your girlfriend said that you don't
Talk to losers like me.
Oh, but if she knew that she
Wasn't your first love.

Your betrayal ate at me
While I was lost in the rain.
Though I began to realize that
I have more power than you.
I don't have to hide who I am.

"All Eyes on Obergefell"

I go to sleep in fear,
But I don't dare shed a tear.
Do I dare look at my phone,
Knowing my anger will rise in my tone?
I keep my eyes open.

All eyes on Obergefell,
Hoping I can stay out of my shell.
They tell me not to worry,
Not to let my vision get blurry.
I keep my mouth open.

All eyes on Obergefell,
As conservatives say I'm going to Hell,
Wishing to flee like a deer.
I keep my hands open.

All eyes on Obergefell,
I feel like I'm caged inside a cell.
Will they overturn it like Roe?
Will I face a new foe?
I keep my breaths open.

All eyes on Obergefell,
In despair, I shall dwell.
If it ends, I'll holler.
I refuse to feel smaller.
All eyes on Obergefell.

For if they overturn it,
We'll throw a fit.
From inside, your world shall be split.
Your eyes will be filled with grit.
All eyes on Obergefell.

A simple right as marriage
Between two consenting adults
Should not be disparaged.
Peace and happiness should be the results.
All eyes on Obergefell.
There will be ringing from a bell.

"No Friend Nor Foe"

Is there something wrong with me?
Am I far too blind to see
The dangers gawking at me?

I try to smile and act
Like the odds are not stacked
Against the matter of fact.

There's no friend nor foe to stop me,
And all I wanna do is flee.
There's no friend nor foe to kill me,
And I'll forever be captured without glee.

I'm not gonna lie,
I've been depressed as hell,
Hoping my emotions won't tell.

Even when I look up at the sky
I still wish to die,
Or wishing I had the courage to be high.

There's no friend nor foe to stop me,
And all I wanna do is flee.
There's no friend nor foe to kill me,
And I'll forever be captured without glee.

I wish I could lie,
Say things are alright,
And not want to cry.
I know better,
For I want to die
As I look up at the sky,
Wondering what life will be like
After I finally die.

Can I tell anyone? Hell no...
It would kill them to know.
I'd rather be torn apart by a crow,
Or walk barefoot in freezing snow.

There's no friend nor foe to stop me,
And all I wanna do is flee.
There's no friend nor foe to kill me,
And I'll forever be captured without glee.

I guess I'll try to smile and act
Like the odds are not stacked
Against the formal pact
That I've now cracked.

My will to continue
Has been attacked,
And I can't face
The harsh impact.

"Lost Charming"

Was the love of my life
Hit by a bus?
Never breathed enough life
To live one with me.

Is this why I'm so lost?
Is this why love's lost to me,
And will never show
It's beautiful and kindly face?

And here's Prince Charming,
So handsomely alarming,
But lost of light when
His eyes meet mine.

There's something wrong with me,
For love's just not my touch.
A life of misery and lonesome
Shall be the only thing here.

They say love happens when you
Least expect it, but I'll never
Experience it. I feel so lost,
And my heart will stop beating...
    Soon.

"Home"

There are no birds chirping in this
Disaster of a realm.
A train's whistle blows in the distance.
Is that you, finally coming home?

A dog was barking and howling at the moon.
Does this mean you'll be home tomorrow?
The old lady down the street asked me
About you, wondering if you had returned,
But I had to frown and shake my head.

I've written to you for the last month,
But I've been met with no reply.
I've sat alone at the kitchen table
For hours on end, reflecting on the life
We said we'd build together.

Tears have filled my eyes when I look
At the photos we took together.
You taught me how to love,
But a piece of me wishes you hadn't.
You were the home for my heart.

Was there something that I did?
Did I push you away,
Say something wrong,
Or did I fail myself again?

One day, a car will come.
I wish it was yours.
Instead it's the sheriff
To tell me that you're dead.

My heart shall die at home
                    with you.

"In the Car"

The sky is falling,
I try to refrain from bawling.

Jamming in my car,
Hoping to travel far.

It's the only way to distract
The thoughts in my mind that have smacked.

Bad news clouds my mind,
But I'm trying to remain kind.

My hands on the wheel
While I'm trying to feel.

Jamming in the car,
What if I hung out in a bar?

Make a mistake or two
To help what I'm going through

Singing in the car,
Hoping the pain won't scar

My foot on the pedal,
Hoping I won't have to backpedal

Will I run out of gas?
Admiring the crack in the glass.

I try to think
About the things that sink.

Hoping not to cry,
And not want to die.

My voice fills with rage,
Trapped inside a cage.

This is how I feel free,
Be out till three.

Screaming in the car,
Hoping no one would hear from afar.

The sky is falling,
And I won't be bawling.

"Dear Little Me"

Dear Little Me,
Don't you dare be afraid.
Don't listen to what they say, and
Be yourself regardless.

Be yourself even if they tell you
That you need to fix that attitude of yours.
Being contrary and feisty
Runs strong in our bloodline.

And when your passion fills your heart,
Don't give in when they say that
"Passion does not bring in
 the big bucks in life."

They'll tell you that
You should enroll in the military,
And you aren't sure why. Don't give in,
Even if they pester you about it,
Unless that's what you want.

When you say that you want a different path,
And they scoff at you, don't give in.
Dear Little Me, always
Follow your heart and don't give in.

Dear Little Me, don't you dare
Fade into the darkness like I did. Not even
When they say that you need to be into sports,
And they overlook that special gift inside of you.

And if anxiety courses through your body, and you
Can't get a single word out, don't
Let them shut down your greatest goals.
Prove 'em wrong and give 'em hell.

If they tell you that you're doomed
Because you're not in STEM, kick them.
And if you are into STEM, then great!
Regardless, you will always matter to me.

Dear Little Me, don't you dare shed a tear.
If they make you feel terrible in any way,
Let them know that they need to clean up their act.
They should have learned that long before now.

Dear Little Me, you are doing so much,
So don't panic about them, because
I will always be proud of you.
I just so happen to know a thing or two.

Dear Little Me, I'll always be proud of you,
Because I lived through all of this,
And if I have a say, you won't.
Dear Little Me, I will always stand by you.

Dear Little Me, because you are strong,
You will forever be special to me.
Dear Little Me, be who you are and never, ever
Become the shadow in the shallows.

"Don't Mourn Me"

Don't mourn me.
I can't see
The silly little truth
When you thought you
Were being smooth.
I can't bear to see this through.

Don't mourn me
After I die.
Mourning won't solve a thing,
Even if all you see
Is misery brought on by
The aura that I bring.

Damn it, damn it!
Is romance dead?
I'm all stuck in a pit,
And it's making me
Feel great dread.
I can't see

The future with you.
I can't believe the words I've read.
Reality is crashing down,
And I don't see a wedding gown.
The spoken truth is dead.
I just hope you see it too.

BOOK II: BLOAT

"Silly Little Game"

I'm surrounded by dirty judgment.
Can't make a choice without you
Knowing my next move.
Who are you to decide my fate?

Is my face too easy to read?
That's alright for the
Writer's Notebook keeps my secrets hidden,
Where no one can touch them.

Is this the only way that I can play
Your silly little game?
My Notebook shall protect me,
And will hide my true nature.

I don't do this because I want
To defy all logic. I'm a rule-follower,
But this is the only way that I can
Stay sane while being at the end.

I cling and I scream,
You might claim that I'm unworthy,
But worthiness is not subjective.
My will shall find a way to live.

I'm surrounded by dirty judgment.
I will plot silently, not letting you
Know my next move
Who are you to decide my fate?
 I'll win this game,
 Even if I lose in the end.

"Thoughts and Prayers"

They're wrapped in a body bag,
On their way to the morgue.
They'll examine the body,
And see that a monster took their life.

The news will say a tragedy occurred here.
The family will say nothing about it.
The monster's name will be released.
And the victim's headstone won't exist.

They're sent off to the funeral home,
Where only a few people will attend.
Some may cry, others may frown,
But they were never dressed in white.

Creators will scream about this tragedy,
And the best that the common person will say
Is, "Thoughts and prayers, thoughts and prayers."
And the news will list their name.

They needed your thoughts and prayers when they were
Still alive, gasping for air in their everyday life.
Killed for existing or killed for no reason,
You can only mutter.

They throw the body into the cremation chamber,
It was slaughtered into fragments.
This was what they wanted, but not in this way.
In a hundred years, they'll be forgotten.

So, tell me why I shouldn't have anxiety
In this cruel ass world?
Try to placate me from my deepest fears,
When all that will be said is "prayers."

I don't give a damn if my words leave you sour.
This is the harshest truth.
I am drowning down with my sorrows in this cruel
World, and it will do nothing but make me suffer.

Where were you when they were alive?
Drinking coffee or reading a headline?
What are you doing as the world goes to hell?
Your thoughts and your prayers won't revive them.

"Shall I Compare You to the Other Boys?"

Shall I compare you to the other boys?
They've told me that you like to break hearts,
But talking to you seems like they aren't your toys.
Perhaps my feelings are like the tip of a dart.

Your perfect hair draws me in,
And your cold blue eyes are so sweet.
Although, I know my feelings can't win,
Because I've been told those muscular guys have me beat.

But something tells me that I should try
To take a chance with you and to see where it goes.
Perhaps I won't tell you how I feel before I die,
But I'll watch you from a distance in your perfect shows.

I envision us walking together through a beautiful place,
And how I would want to hold your hand.
Your spoken words leave the perfect trace,
And our footprints would be left in the sand.

Shall I compare you to the other boys,
Or should I take that leap of faith?
Will I just be one of your toys
Or will I be a man of good faith?

"Darling"

Darling don't fade away,
Don't be on your way.
Darling, I'll plead and cry,
And I'll hope you'll stand by.

Darling, look me in the eye,
And don't make me pry.
Darling, tell me what you think,
Because if you don't, I might sink.

Your blue eyes call to me,
A future for us to see.
Oh Darling, how I want you
To see us through.

Darling, I'll always be sure
That nothing could happen in a blur.
But that doesn't stop me
From wanting to bend on one knee.

Darling, your eyes are so wide.
You look like you've seen a ghost.
You breathe out a sigh,
And you walk away as you say goodbye.

Darling, tell me what you think.
To darkness, I'll blink
And I'll swear to never love again.
I'd love to try to talk to you again.

Darling, you're gone from me.
I was hoping you'd see
What true love was like with me
But I'll forever let you be.

Oh Darling, you lost.
I met someone else who tossed
Their feelings my way,
And with him, I'll stay.

Darling, it's too bad.
Your chance was sad.
He made me happier than
The richest man.

"You're Screaming at Me"

You're screaming at me,
And you won't stop.
Your voice is trembling with
Your hatred.

You're screaming at me,
And it's breaking down the walls.
Tears fill my eyes, and I try not to sob.
Why are you doing this to me?

Is the pain that you feel
Just trying to be directed at me?
Why do you keep doing this?
Why do you wish to demean me?

I cry to make you stop,
But you won't. You ripped
Up my paper with all of my thoughts.
Why won't you listen to reason?

Did I do something to upset you?
Why do you keep coming at me?
You keep screaming at me and
You just won't stop.

Be careful, you'll just lose me,
And in the years that follow,
You'll wonder why.
Don't bother crying about my faults.

What did I do to you to deserve this?
Do I deserve this forever?
What will you do when it's my turn to leave?
Why do you insist on destroying me?

My hand goes into a fist and I stand up,
I look you in the eyes and I say enough.
You cower backward, astonished,
But the hate you present will bite you back.

You were screaming at me,
But now I am screaming at you.
You may say how it's my fault,
But I won't give you the satisfaction.

You forget that your miserable life
Doesn't have to drag people down with you,
And you forgot how to love yourself.
Your hatred will only bite you back.

"Forget it"

A little voice says to me
As he's holding a candy ring,
"When you marry a girl,
You'll give her a big ring like
This one right here."
Emptiness fills my chest,
Pain fills my heart.
Oh, you poor, innocent soul,
If only I could tell you
The biggest truth.

Forced to live everyday under
A lie that they couldn't
Be exposed to, for fear
That I'm "indoctrinating" you.
Always told to say something
When the time's right, but
Perhaps I shall not say anything at all.
I will live a lie for you.

How do I proceed to hide
In the shallows that are my life?
How do I ensure that I won't
Upset the people who claim that
They care about me, but yet
Vote against my existence at the polls?
Do I remain silent, for the
Betterment of this false union?

Even when they say that
I'm pretending to be the silly little
Victim in this madness?

Am I supposed to give up?
Am I supposed to live
A stupid lie that no one believes?
Forget it! Forget it!

My existence doesn't deserve to
be shunned, and you deserve to
Be called out when you vote
against my right to exist.
Even if I must be exiled,
Lost in the woods to write
Gay love stories and poems.

Hell, just forget it.
Forget it like you always do.

"Far Away"

It's the end of an era.
I've given it my all.
I can't keep going,
The walls are closing
Me in, making it hard
For me to breathe.

Every time I'm around you,
It feels like I'm not welcome.
The sinking feeling
Suffocates me.
I know you voted against
My right to exist.

You're afraid that I'm going
To indoctrinate your kids,
So maybe I shouldn't be around
Maybe I'll stay away, far away.
Maybe it's just better this way.

I used to imagine you
At my wedding,
Hoping you'd be by my side
I'm worried that my pride is too hard
For even you to handle.

And there's so much
That lingers in my mind,
Like the times you tried
To be kind to me,
But the memories are lost.

You really wouldn't care
If I wound up dead tomorrow.

It's time for me to hang back.
I need to be distant.
I have to put the genealogy away,
And hope that a descendant will
Continue where I left off.

It's not my job to hold everyone together.
It's my job to control my own life,
And to not be stuck in an untruthful union.

I need to go away, far away.
I need to focus on myself a bit.
I need to restart far away from you.
I need to not worry about
Remaining invisible to please you.

So when you read my book,
I hope you realize
That while I don't blame you for anything,
I still need to take my leave.
For a while, a little while,

In this place that stands far away.

"Courtesy"

Listen here,
Listen close.
We're gathered here today
To say thanks for our blessings.

Courtesy begs at my mind,
While my boyfriend
Stays sweet and kind.
How can I sit here,
Hoping no one would hear
The cussing under my breath?

Election season is over,
And I feared the outcome,
Knowing some of these people
Voted against my rights,
And possibly even theirs.

I would have been consoled,
From the ones that matter most.
They wouldn't bear to
See me down in a rut.

Am I even cared about?
Do I even matter to you?
Even if I did what
The strongest women would have,
How could everyone else
Be so blind?

The dinner table's quiet,
And I want to ask, but I
Have to be the bigger person.
We're gathered here today,
To dine in peace,
Like we always have.

I've spent so many hours of my life
Searching and finding the graves
Of those who came before,
Because I'm the only one who
could bother to give a damn.
Even if these dead people would
Not have agreed with my existence,

I am their successor.

I am the product of
Their terrible mistakes,
The product of
Their misfortunes,
The product of
Their happiness,
The product of
Their inequality,
And the product of
Their lives.

In their shadows, I remain.

Courtesy tries to flee my mind,
But I chose to remain kind.

But for how long?

For in the end, I know
Who I am and I am
A beacon of hope.

"Generosity"

On his deathbed,
An old man voices his dread.
Sure, he had a good life,
He loved his wife,
Loved his kids,
His life matched the perfect bids.

Death approached him,
Not knowing how not to be grim.
"I lived a good life."
"And an afterlife
shall await you."
The reaper attempted to not seem blue.

"Is there something you judge me for?"
The reaper attempted to not roar,
"What should I judge you of?"
"I professed my love
 For those around me.
God's light is all I see."

With a sigh, the reaper sang,
"Oh, but lying flew from your tongue.
You supported fascists that came to power,
Hatred was all that you could shower.
You lied with others, it makes me sour,
With the innocents you attempted to deflower."

"This is all true, dear reaper.
There's no point in lying to the gatekeeper."
"Was it worth it?"
"Not a bit."
The reaper sighed, "I'm sorry.
Generosity is supposed, I'm sorry."

"Don't be, I understand your pain."
"You don't, you can't, your chain,
Your work hurt millions,
So many lost civilians.
Who am I to judge? I guide.
My purpose must be kept wide."

"Before you proceed, where do I
Go? Will I float in the sky?"
The reaper sighed, I don't decide,
I'm just the guide.
The universe decides your fate
On this date."

The reaper held out his hand,
The man attempted to stand.
The reaper tried to smile,
But the man turned into a pile.
He should have known that
The man's fate would have gone splat!

"Prowess"

My words are not dead.
They scream echoes,
They fight battles,
They win.

My words show the happy ending,
They give suspense,
But are they built on imagination
Or are they built on lies?

I cannot tell.
My words, my prowess,
Can not be broken.
Were I to lie if I tried
To be your knight?

They can taunt us, but
I'll always be here to fight.
My muses sing me a lullaby,
My pen at the ready.

My prowess, as strong as a bull,
My blood is as strong as a warship.
My words are powerful
For they are engraved in stone.

"Fidelity"

My love for you transcends space.
It will never be locked into a cage.
It shall never erase.

Cheating on me caused me to brace.
I have to let you perform on stage.
My love for you transcends space.

A new challenge I may face,
I'm swept over with rage.
It shall never erase.

Do I have to run a race?
I can't just turn the page.
My love for you transcends space.

This must be the case.
My love for you can't expire in this age.
It shall never erase.

I can't hit you in the face with a vase.
I can't turn to a new page.
My love for you transcends space,
It shall never erase.

"Honesty"

The written truth is dead.
Though, I shall never lie to you.
My heart has been broken,
It was split into tiny little pieces.
Will you do the same?

I'll tell you the truth,
The whole truth, and nothing but the truth,
But would you do the same?
They say that chivalry is dead,
But I try to embrace it.

I'll tell you the truth,
Some of these poems are lies.
Some, but not all.
If you begin to question,
Then you should approach me.

This is the only way
I can face my fears.
This is cheaper than therapy
And I feel so satisfied to write,
For no one understands me.

I'd hope for the same honesty in return,
For if not, my heart will continue to burn.
My fear runs to the grave,
Through this, I can be brave.
I am my own knight in shining armor.

"I Bet"

I bet you look really
Stupid right now.
I bet it just kills
You to be wrong.
I wonder if I ever
Come across your pathetic
Little mind.

Look at you, you
Stupid miserable wretch.
I bet you think your
Sorry for excuse of a life
Is so damn perfect.

I bet you think that
I was the most disappointing
Thing of your miserable existence.
I hope I was.

But then again, we both know,
I live to make you disappointed.
I whisper to demons in my dreams,
Pleading with them to
Restrain you when you
Come falling down to hell.

Your miserable frame shall be
Ripped apart, limb by limb.
I asked them to drape your
Entrails like a curtain,
Warning the rest of those
Miserable little demons that
Decide to cross my path.

When I was done,
I plotted my revenge.
There is no pleading
For peaceful revenge.
My revenge ascends.

I shall scream from
The rooftops, proving to
The world the truth;
That you are a miserable
Excuse for a man and
A sorry attempt of a human being.

While I remain passive,
Hoping that karma shall deliver,
I hope you remain miserable.
The amount of hatred and anger
Has been long exhausted.

You shall never lay a single hand
Upon my skin, and the day you
Pass from this world will be
The day that I will rejoice!

"The Old and Forgotten Graveyard"

Down that old road,
There lies a place that has been long forgotten.
Who would know what lies here?
While some lie in eternal slumber here.

There lies a place that has been long forgotten,
Some graves broken, some graves lie,
While some lie in eternal slumber here.
It may feel as if someone lurks behind your shoulder.

Some graves broken, some graves lie.
This place seems rather spooky.
It may feel as if someone lurks behind your shoulder,
Do not be filled with anguish, this place is peaceful.

This place seems rather spooky,
That much is true,
Do not be filled with anguish, this place is peaceful.
This graveyard, old and forgotten, still stands.

That much is true,
The back section seems hidden,
covered by a doorway of trees.
This graveyard, old and forgotten, still stands.
So many forgotten souls lie in eternal slumber.

The back section seems hidden,
covered by a doorway of trees.
So many broken graves and fences.
So many forgotten souls lie in eternal slumber.
Will I suffer the same fate after I pass too?

So many broken graves and fences.
It is time to leave, I took the pictures of those I needed.
Will I suffer the same fate after I pass too?
To be lost and forgotten is a terrible fate...

"The Bear"

I don't relate to your pain,
Nor the sorrows built right
Into your shallow core.

Hope and love is what you'll gain
When we express the words we write,
Even though our thoughts are sore.

I wish I could make a difference,
Bring the pain to those who harmed you,
Those who took advantage.

My words are not captured in indifference,
And my actions have not disarmed
Those who are in the advantage.

Thousands of women have suffered
Like you suffered and they feel similar.
Thousands of women, all overlooked.

Secrets remain undiscovered,
Their voices, they remain similar.
Their situations overlooked,
Overlooked by those in power,
And by those who voted for him.

This is part of the reason why
Women would choose the bear.

"Asylum"

The rain hits the road
As I scream and holler.
My voice runs dry, my palms sweaty.
I hate this life, I hate this so much,
So much so that I'd rather end it.
I'd rather end it right now.

The patients have overrun the asylum,
And with that, they've ruined me.
I tried to escape, but I felt trapped.
They've overrun the asylum with me inside it.
I've come so close, yet I feel
Like I'm running in place, lost to dust.

There are no guards here, no safeguards.
All that remains here are the
Crooked and crazy, lost to desolation.
I tried to escape, but no one heard my cries.

I'm lost, lost, lost.
All I want to do is end it now...

Here and now,
In this asylum...

"The One"

The Lost Poem from March 2020

To the one, you know who you are.
To the truth, you know who you are.
To the life that is felt,
when you are who you are.
There is great pain in life,
and it seems to knock many down.
Having to live with a hole in your heart,
knowing that something is missing.

When the truth gets revealed, you feel something.
You feel love or you feel hatred.
This always scares the truth, stretches it.
It can even haunt you.

The pain that is felt always makes you stronger.
You are who you are, and that is the truth.
You are the light to the darkness.
You are the healer to the pain.
You always make things seem better,
But everything will never be the same.

To the one, you make the light feel like home.
To the one, you make everything better.
You are the eye of the storm.
You are the one.

Nothing makes much sense anymore.
Nothing seems to be fixed anymore.
Everyone and everything seem to be destroyed.

But around you, around you,
There is nothing wrong.
You are the one.

"Don't Go to Him"

Don't go to him,
He's crazy.
Don't go to him,
He's nuts.
Don't ask him,
He doesn't know what he's doing.
Don't talk to him,
He's too dumb.
Don't even think about it,
He's a monster.
Don't go near him,
He's dangerous.
Don't anger him,
He'll eat your heart out.
Don't date him,
He's far too crazy.
Ghost him,
He's nothing anyways.

Don't go near his tombstone,
It's cursed.
Don't read his books,
He cursed them.
He was wretched when he lived.
He rests in Hell where he belongs.
Don't go to him,
He's a madman, even in death.
He must be sent to the grave,
For he's far too gone to save.

All eyes on me
For you'll be
Too lost and soon forgotten.
He's got that effect.

Don't bother,
They banned his books for a reason.
There's a reason he's erased,
Ignore what he says he's faced.
Erased from the stone,
Isolated he's placed.
Stay away, far away,
He might turn you gay
Before you have the chance to pray.

Don't go to him,
For his tale is too grim.

"Don't Question Me, I'm a Madman"

They've called me crazy,
But I feel as happy as a daisy.
They say I'm dramatic,
My party is locked in the attic.
Don't question me, I'm a madman.
I hit them on the head with a pan.
I'm drunk on the bottom bunk,
Playing around with a hunk.

Don't question me, I'm a madman.
I ran over my ex with my van,
Let's hope the cops don't find me,
I drowned at sea.
I wanna play around with a cute twink,
Hoping my anxiety doesn't cause me to sink.
Don't question me, I'm a madman,
I'm far too dumb to ban!

Don't question me, I'm a madman,
I've got nothing to plan.
There's a cute twink,
But I'm too drunk to think.
I lost my friend,
My thoughts are too crazy to bend.
Don't question me, I'm a madman,
This party's filled with too many men to scan.
Don't question me, I'm a madman.
I'm gonna make a mistake or two.

"Is It Over?"

Is it over?
I'm left to give the cold shoulder.
I shouldn't have to witness
The burned, dead bridges.
Is it over?
Anguish decides my fate
All because you chose hate.

It's all over...
I welcome depression,
I can't remain sober.
We're back in regression.
They'll say I'm dramatic
When I'm being pragmatic.
Is it all over?

My limpid thoughts
Are the tiny dots
On paper, filled with blood.
Disgrace will follow me,
Drained of my lifeblood.
It's all over, I can't see.

Is it over?
What's the matter with
All of you stupid people?
I wish I could be hungover.
You dare plead the fifth.
I want to jump off a steeple,
Because it's all over...

"Words"

Words, words, words.
All around me are words.
Some spoken, some online.
I vaguely remember of a time,
Where all around me were those
Who were not faint-hearted.
What was it like to not hear the words
Spew from people's mouths?
What was it like not to hear a word?

Words. Words. Words.
And what bloody words they were,
Stuck in my mind like a song stuck in my head.

Words. Words. Words.
How profound!
How rude!
Why do you say such things?
Do you hear yourself?
Do you hear how much of a fool that you sound?

Words. Words. Words.
When countered with an opposite view
You automatically argue.
You can't keep your words to yourself!
You are so lost, so ignorant
To the truth behind other words.
And here I am, forced to hear your words,
While some don't say a thing.
Your words slowly infect my lungs.

They suffocate me from inside.
Your words make my heart
Beat slower and slower,
And yet here I stand, resilient as ever.

The time of a world phenomenon,
And your words did not change.
You make stupid accusations and unreal theories,
And I am forced to hear your words.
Your screams are like that of a banshee,
And I can't help but cower and cover my ears.

Words. Words. Words.
As I long to love all that I have lost,
You do not back down.
You scream in my ears
WORDS! WORDS! WORDS!
WORDS! WORDS! WORDS!
You stupid fool, I am done
With your words, words, words.

Words. Words. Words.
That's it!
I have won!
Though time may go on,
Plagued by insolence and your fake decrees.
I laugh and smile,
And you sigh and frown.
You will not conquer my own...
Words. Words. Words.

I know my power.
I know my strength.
I know my abilities.
I know my gift.
I know the past,
And I know the future.
Through all,
I will continue to fight and I will use my
Words. Words. Words.

BOOK III: DECAY

"With Hope as my Weapon, I Must Try"

You taught me right from wrong,
Taught me to respect those among.
Always strong, paying no mind
To the fake heroes that blow in the wind.

Our bond was too tough to move,
Around you, I felt nothing but love.
You denied a throne,
All ill intentions had gone.

The path ahead is rough,
And I need you to not take the dough.
I need you to try
To not be influenced by their chemistry.

I've ranted endlessly to my lover,
Hoping my bond with you isn't over.
I can't stand seeing you in a red hat,
Wishing I could win you over in Baccarat.

I feel so lost,
You've lost your outpost.
If freedom can be lost to chemistry,
Then with hope as my weapon, I must try.

I may be left alone in the frost,
But I'll play it safer than most.

"I Might Be Aloof"

I might be aloof
But I'm not creating a spoof.
My hands are tied,
The hole in my heart is too wide.
I think I'm going crazy
Or perhaps I'm just too lazy.

I look at the manuscripts,
Escaped from the most dangerous crypts.
How can I go on?
My inspiration dare goes gone.
Perhaps if I experienced love
For myself, it would fit like a glove.

I might be aloof,
But I can also be a goof.
I don't know where to go.
I wish I had money to blow.
I wish I could secure the dough,
But all of it's not what I know.

I might be aloof,
Best to leave my life childproof.
I wish I could dance to stars
And go have fun at bars.
I wish I could be a film star,
Or drive over a dude with my car.

I could be standing through a sunroof,
Standing to deny the proof.
I could invent a time machine,
Wishing I could remain clean.
I could have myself thrown,
Wishing I could finally let out a moan.

I might be aloof,
And all this might be a spoof.
I have found it hard to move,
Impossible to find my groove.
I just want to feel like a teen
All over again while my body lacks green.

"In All My Life"

I'm so nervous,
I'm gonna be a wreck.
I'm worried this won't end well
And he's gonna hate me.
Will he turn away at the sight of me?

I meet his eyes,
And see his beautiful hair.
I'm getting more and more nervous,
But when he speaks,
I was drawn right in.

Our conversation was just so magical,
Geeking out to nonsense and
Laughing to hilarious jokes.
My hands were shaking,
Calming down to his beautiful personality.

The night had to end eventually,
But I'd have stayed with him.
A goodbye with a smile, thinking
This was the best I've felt
In a long damn time.

In all my life,
Nothing has gone the way
It's supposed to.
On this one simple night,
One thing went right.
It was such a magical night,
Left smitten and so soft,
Wishing to plan the next date.
In all my life, nothing had
Gone right, always messed up.

In all my life,
This was it, he's the
Man of my dreams, and here
He finally shows his face to me.

God, how do I tell him that
He's the one for me?

"The Chime"

Every time I hear the chime,
My heart skips a beat.
You brighten my day from the grime,
Wondering when we'll next meet.

From the moment that I first
Laid my eyes onto you, I knew
That you were the love of my life.

Every time that I see you,
My heart wants to bust.
Excitement began and it grew,
How desperately I
Want you in my real life.

My nerves are so heavy
Every time that I see you.
I'm not gonna screw this up, am I?

I want to be with you, but
At the same time,
I'm scared that I'll
Make a terrible mistake with you.

How do I respond when I hear
The chime from my phone?
I'm so scared I'll respond in fear,
Worried about everything that
They decided to vote for.

What is the future?
Will it be repaired by a suture?

"Unity"

I want to see your face

Admiring your green eyes
Dreaming that you'll touch me
Often pondering about us
Romance is my passion
Excitement fills me

Yearning for a future with you
Overlooking my obligations
Unity is all I hope for

"Your Face"

I was nothing more
Than a lonely poet
Before I met you.

I concocted poems and stories
Of what could've been,
Hoping I'd meet the wonderful
Prince Charming.

In a way, I did.
I took lost love, and
I ran with it.

I imagined the perfect
Man, filling the wildest vision.
Building a world, filled it.

All of this, always thinking
That the one for me must've
Been hit by a car.

Now, all I think of
When I imagine my imaginary love interests,
I only see a single thing,
And that is your face.

"You and Me"

I wanna see
You and me.
Holding hands,
Listening to our favorite bands.
Blushing cheeks,
Between two geeks.

I want there to be an "us,"
Where no one would beat us.
With you and me
Strong we'll be.
We'll talk about our projects,
And our most prized objects.

It didn't show, my grave anguish,
My demons I couldn't vanquish,
But it didn't matter.
For you I climbed a ladder,
Seeing it through,
And meeting you.

For I thought my life's plot,
In my anguish which I thought
Would lead me straight to the grave.
You were the only thing that can save,
That which made me feel alive.
I want you and me to thrive.

I wanna see me and you.
My heart was once blue.
Talk to me about your day,
Together, we'll be gay
We can play games together,
And tough through the weather.

My feelings for you can't be buried,
They will always be carried
Of what could be
Between you and me.

"We Were Driving"

We were driving
In the country,
With your hand on my thigh.

We were driving
In the country,
When you joked to me.

What's the future
Of us in this world?
I wanna spend it with you.

We were driving
In the country,
Talking about current events.

Is it uncertain or locked?
With the eye of uncertainty,
I pulled the car over.

I put the car in park,
Taking off my seatbelt
And I whispered in your ear.

No one's taking you away from me.
I'll never let you go,
For my hands will throw.

A kiss on the cheek,
And a hug made me feel
That good old electric shock.

You're there every time that
I forget that I'm not
Anguished to the grave.

We were driving,
My heart beats and my breaths
Are not shallow.

Even if the future is lost,
I know you're there,
Regardless of cost.

With you, my anguish fades,
Cut up by the touch of your blades,
We made it out alive.

"Am I...?"

Am I the drama?
Am I in the wrong
For speaking out?
You're wondering why
I'm so depressed all the time,
But my fear only came true.
Hours and hours of my life
Were wasted all because you're
So high and mighty on your throne.

Am I in the wrong
For wanting a family to come
Home to over the holidays?
Am I in the wrong
When part of my family
Isn't even talking to the others?
I get you're stressed out,
I would be too, but you're
The one causing all the drama.

Am I to blame
For all the grudges and turmoil?
It was only a matter of time
Before the family would fall out of prime.
Perhaps I should have stayed away
From the graves of those who
Whisper my name.
You can never place blame
On a curious, but determined mind.

It took a while,
But I've come to the conclusion
That your behavior isn't savable,
Not bothering for any holidays nor
My point of success that you've
Always doubted me for.
I hope it was worth it.
You'll be old and alone someday.
It's **NOT** my fault.

It's only yours.
You're the only one to blame.
Enjoy your new life, and
Don't come crying to all of us
When it all goes sideways.
I'm not to blame this time.

"Fear is Eating at Me"

Fear is eating at me,
I can't let it be.
What if he ghosts me,
Leaving me alone at sea?

I can't let it be.
My heart wants to be free,
Leaving me all alone at sea.
What if he holds the key?

My heart wants to be free,
Love and devotion is all I see.
What if he holds the key?
What if he ghosts me?

Love and devotion is all I see.
My fear and self-doubt control me.
What if he ghosts me?
What if he leaves me?

My fear and self-doubt control me.
I'm far too worried.
What if he leaves me?
Fear is eating at me...

He didn't ghost me...

"Better than Most"

Is it over?
Are you no longer my lover?

I'm feeling lost,
Deserted at my outpost.

I did something terribly wrong.
I made a mistake among

Something else in mind.
My heart blew away in the wind.

Your beautiful eyes are gone,
No one sits on our throne.

I write poetry
As I look up at the sky.

I wish we had true love,
But my blood does not move.

If only we could try
To test our chemistry.

Perhaps our love won't survive the frost,
But that's still better than most.

"Mythical"

Too many stories in your head,
Don't let it cause you any dread.
Eric nodded and continued to write,
Knowing his work can bite.
His cousin would read what he
Had left behind, what can he be?

What about a map?
Normally, that'd be a load of crap,
But she let him cause a storm.
The thoughts began to swarm.
She always hated science fiction,
But she was too impressed by his diction.

A map of another world,
A story he had uncurled.
Grandma and mom were impressed.
A writer they'd blessed.
From that moment on,
A story had been drawn.

Mythical was born,
After seven years, it'd be torn.
After the death of his grandmother,
The story would be replaced by another.
Don't worry, for in the strife,
Mythical will come back to life.

"The Stories Surround Me"

The stories surround me,
Haunting me every step of the way.
Distractions will solve nothing.

Anguish will only follow me
Throughout my life.
The thoughts scratch my skin.
Ghosts whisper their stories.

The town stood against him.
Shallows are surrounding him.
In this Hell, colors are void.
This must be the end.
Shadows always reside in darkness.

Darkness has a name,
Glad to tell his story.

Bridge to the past tells all.
Finding the words in my brain.
Months may pass before they speak.

"Two Men"

There's two men deeply in love,
Their hearts flying through the skies above.
They gaze at their phones and they ponder,
Hoping that they can grow fonder.

Meet me in the park,
We'll carve in the tree bark,
Our simple, but true feelings,
Later we can paint the ceilings.

There's two men
Across journeys they've been.
Now they get the ability
To live in tranquility.

There's two men
That get to dwell in a den.
They get to forge a life together,
Bearing an unbreakable tether.

There are two men
Whose faith is restored again.
Together their strength
Shall withstand hate's length.

"Do I Deserve This Fate?"

Do I deserve this fate?
Clouded by a wall of hate,
The man of my dreams is gone,
Erasing my hope that was drawn.
It's painful to lose him,
My heartstrings look too grim.
I can never fall for anyone,
Never to be with someone's son.

Do I deserve this fate?
Thinking back to our dates,
And crying myself to sleep.
Memories I hope to keep.
Left to be alone,
Needing to watch my tone.
Rarely hearing the chime,
It's me stuck in time.

Our unity is dead,
It fills me with dread.
It scares me to never see your face again,
Wondering where you've been.
There's no you and me,
It's all gone to sea.
We'll never go driving,
I'll never be thriving.

Do I deserve this fate?
I wish we could have a blank slate.
I've lost you,
The hope's gone blue.
I wish you'd come back to me,
I want us to be.
It's all over,
My anguish spilled over.

"For My Heart, You Hold the Key"

Oh shit!
This is all my fault!
My heart is split,
My wound filled with salt.
I don't know how to go on,
Looking at the hearts I've drawn.

I screwed this up,
My tears filling up a cup.
You're blaming yourself,
While I'm blaming myself.
Come back to me,
I want us to be.

I tried to fight for us,
Your feelings were hit by a bus.
I need you to fight for me,
Our love is what I need to see.
They're telling me it's not meant to be,
But for my heart, you hold the key.

A goodbye message will
Do nothing but keep us still.
You've been gone for a few hours,
All that's left are dead flowers.
Come back to me,
For my heart, you hold the key.

"Are We?"

I don't want tonight
To end just yet.
A hug and a kiss goodbye
Electrified me back to life.

Looking at your bright smile
Sends warmth down my spine.
Are you the one for me?
Are we meant to be?

Are We?

I look back at the faded memories,
I'm lost in their calls.
You made me feel so happy,
But now I feel so crappy.

I screwed this up,
But is there still hope?
Are we meant to be?
Are we going to fix this?

Are We?

"I Want to Live for You"

My heart's been shattered.
I think of your face,
And I'm left feeling all
Hollowed out again.

I know that you said that
I didn't lose you and
That there's nothing that
I did wrong,

But I'm still left feeling
Like I could have prevented
All of this from happening.
It's tough to love you from far away.

You hold the key to my heart,
Your words echo in my brain over and over.
I'm more of a catch than I realize,
But I want to be your catch.

I want to be your duke,
While being the King of Death,
And a masterful scribe
Of undying dogmatism.

Truth is, I felt dead
Up until I met you.
My heart was frozen,
Void of purpose or feeling.

I've shed so many tears
While thinking about you.
I stayed up until midnight,
Crying and screaming, asking,

Asking for God to send you
Back to me, to undo everything
That had just happened.
That was when I heard the chime.

Fate brought us together,
And it's hold stays.
I have to play my cards right,
And hope they don't become reversed.

I have to keep hope alive,
In order to not be sent to
My grave that awaits me.
I want to live for you.

"Regress/Progress/ Regress/Progress"

I've spent so much time
Feeling like I was stuck in slime.
I made progress,
I'd regress
    Regress
        Regress.
I made progress,
    I'd regress.
        Regress.
        Regress.
Do I need to digress?

I made progress.
But I'd regress.
        Regress
          Regress.
I made progress.
        Progress.
        Progress.
But at the end of the day,
I'd only regress.
        Regress.
          Regress.
Do I need to make a guess?
Time keeps passing on,
But I wish I could be gone.

New place, new time,
But I'm still not worth a dime.
I made progress,
Progress, progress.

At the end of the day,
I only felt like I
   Regressed,
      Regressed,
         Regressed.

Am I too hard on myself?
I feel like I'm frozen on a shelf.
I made more progress,
        Progress,
         Progress,
But my dreams felt hollow,
It's too tough to swallow.
I have to pick myself up,
My hope I have to cup,
I have to keep making
Progress, progress, progress,
Even if I feel like I
Regressed, regressed, regressed.

Keep going on, hoping to reach bliss
As he screams, "You got this!"
I do!
Do I?
I do!

I'll make progress, progress, progress.
Even without you by my side,
Determination will be my guide.

"Broken"

It's been a long and terrible while,
My heart is all spread out over the tile.
If I feel this way, thinking that this was my fault,
I can only imagine how you're feeling right now.

Are you being kind to yourself?
Are you eating?
Are you sleeping?

I know that I lost you,
But I still care about you.
I'm hoping that you are not
Taking it all out on yourself.

I care about you far too much,
Be kind to yourself, cherish yourself.
I don't want you to feel broken like I have felt.
If it's meant to be between us, *it will be.*

"I'll Find My Prince Soon"

I'll find my prince soon.
Our love shall be undying.
Now's not the right time.

BOOK IV:
SKELETONIZATION

"Waste of Space"

It's getting late,
And I've got so much on my plate.
My life feels miserable,
And my feelings are inconsiderable.

After all, I'm just a waste of space,
I wish I had my own place,
Far away from here,
Where no one would appear.

I am a burden on all I meet,
And I'd rather lie dead in the street.
They think I asked for this,
But I wish my life would miss.

I'm just a waste of space,
I wish I wasn't such a disgrace.
Every time I cause someone dread,
I only wish that I was dead.

Wishing I hadn't been born,
My heart's been stabbed by a thorn.
I toss my belongings into a fire.
I wish I could cut my own wire.

But I can't...

I'm a burden on all I meet,
Darkness follows when I greet,
I've never been good enough,
And I wish I could act tough.

How miserable am I?
Scared for death to meet my eye,
But too tired to be alive.
From a rooftop, I wish I could take a dive.

I'm just a waste of space,
My life is too strong to erase.
Every time I feel dread,
I just wish I was dead.

Everybody would be better off,
If I lie there as the train takes off.
My life started from a single wish,
I wish I died as a fish.

After all, I'm just a waste of space.
I wish I was bludgeoned with a mace.
All my life, I've never wanted to be alive,
But here I am forced to thrive.

Every time we're faced with death,
I wish it with my dying breath
That it was me instead
Of the person who was dead.

I've always hated my life,
I wish someone would just stab me with a knife.
For me to live is a crime.
It's me, stuck in time.

"I Have to Remain Strong"

This cruel ass year is ending.
I'm upset about the hell that's coming.
I can remain strong.
I have to.
It doesn't matter what happens,
Even if I want to commit murder.
I can keep going,
Even if my heart is broken,
For it's better than being dead.
I am a busy man.
I am an anguished man,
One who has to keep going on,
Even if I imagined a
Different timeline for us.

I have to remain strong,
Even if the man of my dreams
Isn't mine to claim.
I have to remain strong,
Even if this family has been
Torn apart by foolishness.
A smirk on my face can
Hide the pain I feel,
No one can tell.
I'll finish what I started.
The nightmares that gawk at me,
Hoping I'd speak.
Although I'm anguished,
My life won't end this way.

"A Tombstone with Words Written in Stone"

That feeling of hopelessness that clouds my judgment,
Is so surreal as I do my duty times a hundred.
I search, I plot, I travel, and I take
A picture worth a hundred words,
The beautiful scenery that I take in while
I hear a thousand birds.
A tombstone with words written in stone,
A depiction of what remains that I get to decipher alone.
A genealogist is what I call myself,
But a writer is what I'll be.

I watch the world move on,
With that feeling of hopelessness
That clouds my judgment.
Some will say that what I do is rather repugnant,
But if I were gone for hundreds of years,
I would want someone to be all ears.
I will write thousands of words that many will see.

The words are the lives of those who stood before me.
The duty I promised is so surreal, and I must atone,
For those who come next are those who shall throne.
Every single person on this Earth has a story,
And even though our lives are short,
Our stories shall forever be endless.

We will stand forever in our glory.
Writers with a story to tell, we shall be.
I will write every story that I can blurt.
Stories will forever be endless,
And this will be tremendous!

A tombstone with words written in stone,
Surrounded by pure beauty that comes from nature.
If I didn't do this, no one would, forever alone.
It took so long for me to be mature,
And to fully appreciate the world for what it really is.
A depiction of what remains makes it this.

When they look back at the work that I continued,
They will not stand in repulsion,
They will instead learn the truth
Of the history that lies in the past.
The fate of the future will not stand in hell
As long as we contributed
And as the genealogist, my truth is that I shall last.
My gift will not be a victim of expulsion.
Those from the past will never be forgotten.

But at the end of the day, I will still say *adieu*.

"i buried the dreams i had / of us in the backyard"

i buried the dreams i had
of us in the backyard
where no one can touch them now
buried beneath the dirt and snow
never to see the light of day
i can't hear the words they say

i buried the dreams i had
of us in the backyard
where they can never hurt me
i played a game of risk
just to distract my mind
my heart is pure and kind

i buried the dreams i had
of us in the backyard
where they can never make me cry
hoping that i won't have to lie
i had to do this
so i can finally let go

i buried the dreams i had
of us in the backyard
knowing i still hold my card
i got tired of imagining what could be
when i'm flying free

i buried the dreams i had
of us in the backyard
walking it right to the afterlife
wishing it wasn't the end
does this make me the bad guy
knowing that i can't try

though it's said and done
the deed is done
and i'm left here all alone
i don't dare look at my phone
knowing i'll wander right back to you
wishing you'd see us through

is this the story of my life
always struck by a knife
it's the end of our story
it lacks all the glory
and instead lies dead
in the backyard

i buried the dreams i had
of us in the darkness
where the memories
can't haunt me now
i think i'll take a bow
this is the end of the fairytale

"I Want You to Prove Me Wrong"

I want you to prove me wrong
As my heart was broken.
I want you to prove me wrong
When I think that I'm not meant
To fall in love.

I want you to prove me wrong
When you read the tragic poems that
I wrote about my love for you.
I want you to prove me wrong.
I want you to bring me back to life.

Prove me wrong
As the world is ending.
Prove me wrong
When I'm worried that I won't
Have a future with you.

I want you to prove me wrong
When I say that it can't work again.
I want you to prove me wrong
When everyone tells me that
You're not the one.

I want to see you again.
I want to love you.
I want to be by your side,
Navigating through Purgatory
As we fight fascism together.

I want you to prove me wrong.
Dig up those dreams that I had of us
That I buried in the backyard.
Expose them back into the light,
And hold them close to my heart.

Whisper in my ear and tell me
That I've got this.
Be my duke, and together,
We'll rule on our throne.
We'll prove to the world that love exists.

I want you to prove me wrong
When I said that I deserve the darkest fate.
Prove to me that our unity isn't dead.
I want you to prove to me that we can figure this out.
I want to see you and me.

Come back to me and prove me wrong,
Because I have a hunch
That I still hold the key to your heart.
I want you and me to rule the day,
And together we'll be gay.

Will you prove me wrong?
All you have to do is choose me.

POEMS THAT ALMOST MADE THE CUT
FOR *THE HOLLOWED DREAMS*
"A New Day"

It's a brand new day,
And I hope I won't be questioned.
I shouldn't care about what they say,
But their hazards were gestured.

I wake up in my life,
But of course, something is gonna go wrong.
Their words slice into me like a knife,
and I have to tell myself to remain strong.

What is it that sets me apart?
Is it my skin, the darkness of my eyes?
Is it the blood that pumps from my heart?
Is it my size or is it just a surprise?

Perhaps it's my name, a name plagued
By a sorry excuse for a man and a father,
But not an ounce of excuse is made
For not being made too proper.

They all point to my name,
Mispronounce it too many times to count,
But that's okay because I fail to claim
And recognize those on that account.

They can even laugh at "Feeps"
For it's also unheard of, problematic even if
They continue to give me the creeps.
It's making me feel all too stiff.

Get my name out of the pervert's mouth,
It never belonged there either.
I can just feel all of this going south.
I'm going to need a breather.

What will it take?
Must I shorten my name to make you all happy?
Maybe I could do something that could make
Or break this problem to make me less snappy.

They can butcher my name, erase it from history,
But they will never stop me from rising into
Something beyond just a tiny little mystery.
Mythical knows that I will never be broken in two.

My name may make you wonder,
But I will remain fierce and strong.
I will make my name under
My own terms before long.

Get ready for what I'm about to do,
For his name is out,
For I have thought this through.
I made it through the drought.

It's a brand-new day,
And the old me is dead.
Oh, and how I know it causes great dread,
But what remains will be a new Day.

"He Was and He Is"

He was eleven and he had just concocted a story,
Knowing very well that it wasn't the best of quality,
But he kept his ambition alive. At twelve, he didn't
Stop writing, always hoping to make it, not knowing
What would even happen next.

He was thirteen when he kept his ambition alive,
Not slowing down, even when his cousin died.
At fourteen he realized he had a secret, couldn't
Keep it away from anybody. Threatened to stop
Writing, thinking that the world was just ending.

At fifteen, his secret came out, always told to be
Careful as there'd be no turning back after this.
Went from book one to book seven,
And he didn't dare to slow down, even though
These books were so terribly small.

At sixteen, he not only got his license, but he kept
Writing. He went from book seven to book twelve,
And he couldn't stop, even if those books weren't
The greatest. He was seventeen when he finished
Book fourteen, feeling burnt out.

He was eighteen when he realized that he was
Always writing in the background and never gave
Himself a break. Only a few people in his family had
Ever known that he had this gift and that he was
Creating these books from nothing. He was also
Eighteen when he lost his grandmother,

And he was also eighteen when he got so
Depressed that he felt like nothing but a shadow in
The corner and that sparked an idea, an idea that
Lived, but then died when a pandemic came around.
Even in death, it was never the end.

At nineteen, the boy became a genealogist,
Obsessed with the stories of the dead due to the
Death of his inspiration, and he got his first job.
Writing a story was a distant memory, with
A brilliant product shelved with its despair.

And he was twenty, just transferred colleges, no
Ending in sight. Gave up on writing and focused on
The degree, hoping that it would make sense
Eventually. He was twenty-one when
He realized he could have hope again.

And at twenty-one, he just finished that book at
36,000 words, wondering about how publishing
Works. At twenty-one, he thought about his pastime
Of death, and a nagging idea came forth.
Now guess what?

He was twenty-two,
Completed the second story, circling back to the
First one, thinking about how he can tie them to an
End. Even while he's about to graduate college, he's
Not going to give up just yet,
For he's only twenty-two.

And while he keeps moving on,
The original fourteen books of nonsense
Never left his mind. He's looked back at what he's
Done, and admired how far he's gotten. A gentle
Reminder calls in his ear; he's only getting started.

While he's only begging to be free
From his current duties.
Something amazing happened,
He published a poetry book
Filled with the perfect hooks.
Twenty-one miseries with
Twenty-one dreams.

Finally opening up to his craft,
He continued working on his books,
Hoping to concoct the perfect hooks.
While the end is getting closer into sight,
He hasn't lost this fight.
He will prevail, and he will never back down,
Because *The Hollowed Dreams* are
Almost over, and they will never cause him
To feel anguish ever again.

And here he is.
Hitting Magna Cum Laude,
Writing through doomsday,
Learning how to teach,
With a ton of goals in reach.
He's so close to the finish line,
Hoping to remain fine.

He's almost free,
Free to reach the real world.
So never mind the clutter
As his heart continues to flutter.
Ignore the tragedies.
Ignore his endless rantings.

He is now twenty three,
Who knows what's next.
Could be a new book,
Could be a new hook,
But it doesn't matter yet,
For he's only twenty-three.

"I Made It This Far"

Is this the tune that
Covers over my tuneless life?
I'm screaming like a bat,
And it has me cowering.

I should rip off the badge,
But fear is striking me, and
It won't escape with a cough.
They told me that I wouldn't make it.

They told me that my anxiety would
Get to me, and I would give up.
Some just flat-out doubted me,
Saying that I wasn't built for it.

But I kept moving forward,
For I live to prove people wrong.
I got this, mark my word,
And if I fail, it'll be my end.

I made it this far, so
There's no going back.
I refuse to trudge on their tar,
For I'm faking it till I make it.

"Is this spite talking or is it
Your real desire to succeed?"
My heart beats. At its pit,
It knows what it wants.

I made it this far,
And I'm not giving up.
I keep making progress,
Even when they said I wouldn't.

They told me that I couldn't make it,
Some have even asked me if I dropped out
When all I did was get a part-time job.
I made it this far, did I not?

Eventually, I grew tired of
All the doubts and whispers.
I found a pastime amongst the dead,
where no one would harm me.

But when one hangs with the dead,
They stir up old stories, stories
That are supposed to be long dead,
But I made it this far.

I kept moving forward, learning
As much as I could, getting smarter
Along the way.
Here I am almost to the finish line.

What are they gonna do when I walk
Across that stage in December?
Is anyone going to be proud,
Or is anyone going to be disappointed?

I fail to care either way, for the
Truth is that the only opinion that
I care about would be my own.
I made it this far, and I refuse to give up.

So take my story if you would,
Spread it across those that are giving up.
Just because some people can stand against you,
Doesn't mean that you should give up.

POEMS THAT WERE PREVIOUSLY
PUBLISHED ONLINE

"My Style"

From the Big Apple to Hollywood.
They say that we are so apathetic.
That there stands no good,
And most men are so unsympathetic.

Who said that we had to not care?
Who said that I can't be a gentleman?
And I have to use fashionable wear.
Kindness will always be my secret medicine.

I really only fall under one stereotype.
I wear what I want but I walk fast.
I guess you could just say that I'm just that type.
Perhaps manners and kindness
Were just left in the past.

They say chivalry is a lost art,
And that people are just jerks.
However, I feel as if everyone's got their part.
My anxiety will always be what lurks.

Stereotypes and labels do not define me,
And the only thing I'll be shrouded by are words.
For as long as I can breathe, I see
I will always be guided by my works.

My style will never be typical,
But my anguish will drive me forward.
If I remain myself, that will be a miracle.
I'll forever keep moving onward.

"Enlighten Me and Trace Your Lines"

It happened again.
I am so tired each and every time.
I am treated like dirt beneath your shoe,
And my fury burns inside my heart.

How am I different than you?
Do I look funny to you?
Are my eyes just too dark
For you to consider me human?

You ask me my nationality
Like I'm somehow foreign.
My name is abnormal,
And you say it like it's shameful.

You point out my skin tone,
Like you're foraging for details.
You say that my face is shaped funny,
And that my ears are like theirs.

Who are they, those you compare me to?
Why do you request to talk to me
Like I am an animal who doesn't belong here?
What exactly is your problem?

Little do you know that my blood runs deep,
It traces back to even before the foundation
Of this country that we stand in.
Little did you know that you're a stupid fool.

My ancestors fought for this country,
They stood firm in their beliefs.
Their blood was on the battlefield.
Their blood is my blood.

The one was a founding trustee,
Another was a minuteman,
And another was a farmer.
They each fought so that we could live.

Notice my word was "we."
This is a place made of equals.
We all have blood in our veins,
Mine is just kinder than yours.

And if I was from a different place,
How would that make me any different?
Perhaps you're too busy having your head
Stuck up where the sun doesn't shine.

Trace your lines like we did,
And put hours of your life into hoping
The next generation doesn't grow
Up to be so ignorant like you.

Trace your lines,
And you'd find that your
Ancestors didn't originally
Come from here.

Boy, would they be so proud?
That you were the outcome of
Their hardships in life.
Enlighten me once you go humble yourself.

"Redemption for Myself"

I fell in love with a boy,
But he was so lame.
I had to ask myself,
"What exactly was I doing?"

My feelings were bold enough to destroy,
And I only had myself to place blame.
He had to keep pushing himself,
In order to make me believe
That he was worth pursuing.

Redemption clouded my mind,
I came to realize that I needed to learn
To truly understand who I was,
And who I am meant to be.

To look back on it now illustrates that I was so blind,
And that I needed to fight for the life that I should earn.
My life is so complicated all because
I need to learn about who I am meant to be.

I am not a people-pleaser,
I am not a boy who fades into the background.
I will seek redemption for myself,
And I will slowly relearn my gift that I once lost.

They warned me about being placed in a freezer,
But they forgot that I am not
Someone who can be pushed around.
To seek redemption for oneself,
Will be something that will not bring a cost.

I fell in love with a boy,
But he was not the one.
I have to ask myself over and over again,
What is it that I deserve for myself?

I laugh and cackle,
For my words have transcended.
I have risen back up from the dead,
And no one will stop me now.

"My Art"

The only art I could produce
Was stories from the dead.
These were my only treasure,
And they were held close to my heart.

My words were far too loose.
Writing was met with much dread.
But there was a boy with whom I felt pleasure.
His whole world was surrounded by art.

I thought he was so perfect.
We'd spend hours talking, but he'd grow
To be distant when I wanted to meet.
He shot me down every time.

When he didn't answer, I was wrecked.
His true colors began to glow.
I'll try to keep dancing to this beat.
When I least expected it, my words began to climb.

My gift is back and I
tell him, but he pouts.
He lost his own gift,
And I wanted to help him.

But his morality began to pry.
From him the truth sprouts.
My feelings for him had to drift.
My words were all too grim.

The very next day, I got an email.
I got published for the very first time.
My art came back into the world,
And I get to share it all around.

He's not published but I am.
I will publish my works
And that is magical.
My art is worth more than he'll ever be.

"For Amanda;"

If I could,
I'd write a poem for you.
If I could,
I'd tell a tale to you.

If I could,
I'd give the world,
To be able to see you smile.
But it's too late.

It's been too late.
How the world would
Have been so different if
You were here today.

Tears fill our eyes,
Wondering about what could
Have happened.
But I'll tell you what can happen.

I'll write a poem for you,
Sure. But is that enough?
It's not. It never will be,
Because even I can't do enough.

So I'll not just write a poem,
I'll write a story.
I'll mean every single word,
And I will do my part.

So I did, I wrote a story for you,
And that's not enough,
Because I'll even create a world for you.
I would trade every ounce of my gift for you.

Sitting around won't change a thing,
And though I could never bring you back,
I will never stop writing for you.
My gift is your gift, and it always will be.

No, I can't bring you back,
But if my words make every single
Person out there feel the light
In the darkness, then so be it.

No one deserves to feel the pain that
We felt nine years ago.
And though you are gone from us,
Your story isn't over just yet;

So, Amanda, for you,
I wrote a story.
And how I wish you would be able
To read its words.

Deep in my heart,
I hope you know,
That you are never going to be forgotten.
I will dedicate every single word to you.

"Goodbye"

I wanna travel back to when I was younger.
Back to when you were better.
Back to the days when you'd be grumpy.
Back to the days when your house was home.

It only took for you to be in
Poor health to finally say the words.
The words no one would ever hear.
To finally say, "I love you."

We all know why you'd never say it.
You were trying to be abrasive in order
To not show the pain you were feeling.
But your humanity continued to show.

When you had everything to live for,
But it all was swept away in one moment.
You welcomed death with open arms,
Only to realize that it wasn't right.

You changed your mind last second,
And it made us cry in the night.
There's nothing anyone could do.
You had been through hell.

You welcomed death but changed
Your mind at the last second.
You realized that you had everything to live for.
There was nothing that anyone could do.

And when death finally came, I hoped
That you were finally able to see
Everyone that we had lost before,
And I hoped that you hugged them tightly.

I wanna go back in time
To where we were so happy.
To the days that we all had you.
But those days are long gone.

I never got to say goodbye,
Only to visit you from time to time,
My eyes filled with tears every time.
I wish I could have made you proud.

If there's a life after this one,
I hope you know that I am trying,
And that your hard work never went to waste.
But I still wanna go back to say goodbye.

"Fearful"

Don't attempt to make me fearful.
Because being fearful has never
Solved a single thing, and I refuse
To give in to the greatest fear.

While the darkness makes me tearful
And I am forced to use a faulty lever,
I slowly make an attempt to deduce.
The words are forming in order to be clear.

The panic is creeping in.
The Reaper holds his scythe around the corner.
He's coming for me and I keep
Still, knowing that he can't win today.

I throw my doubts and fears into a tin.
He holds back his tears like a poor mourner.
His shallow breaths can't be held and begins to weep.
Perhaps, he won't worry so much someday.

I'll extend my hand to him,
And I will pull him in close to my heart.
Goodbye fear, go bother someone else.
The Reaper is a gentle soul who means to be sacred.

His smile is not grim.
It came from masterful art.
Feelings chime with the ringing of bells,
And they won't become unpaired.

So don't try to make me fearful.
I'll stand firm in my stance, just as I did before.
While I shouted my fears from the rooftop,
I will never lose track of the hope in my heart.

"I Wish We Could Meet Across the Stars"

I wish we could meet across the stars,
So I could feel your sweet embrace.
Our distance feels like a great set of bars
Stuck in our way, it's too tough to trace.

I look at and I mock my rough draft,
My words all tangled in my despair.
They float down a river like a raft,
And they're too hard to bear.

My love for you will transcend time and space.
I'll wait for you in my own little Purgatory,
Where I hope you will welcome my embrace.
It's so strange how this matches my story.

I reached my goals for this story
And I hope that the next steps are clear.
Here lies my portion in all its glory,
And I shall own it from the rooftops, without fear.

The reaper can always stalk me, hoping to
Make his greatest move, but I don't fall
For tricks that easily. That much is true.
I like to take my time, enough to stall.

I look at my word count, and I close my computer,
And I feel like an accomplished newsman.
The former man of my dreams became a suitor,
While we could be *Death and the Groomsman*.

"In God's Name..."

Originally published in the Student Literary Journal,
Allusions, by Indiana State University

I could stand here,
While you stand near.
Your fiery eyes boggle
Showing details that toggle
Your truest personality filled with fear.

I could stand here,
Seeing you be filled with fear.
Are you trying to mock me?
Are you afraid to let it be?
In God's name, I still stand here.

You shout, you cry, you attempt to punish.
In God's name, you attempt to banish.
I smile, you frown, I laugh, you groan,
Mockery filled with disdain unworthy to throne,
In God's name, I'd be better off alone!

Regardless of all you've done,
You still think you get to shun.
Open arms, you hope your God will be,
But a frown and disapproval
Will be what you see.
Your fate shall be held dual.

To mock, but atone
For great atrocities unknown,
You will be refused
To Hell, you'll be reduced.
In God's name, I swear it be true.

In God's name, you only knew,
You shall burn alone,
Take your fascist buddies with you,
And maybe - just maybe it's true.
In God's name, I say *adieu.*

"Fates That You May Never Know"

Originally published in the Student Literary Journal, *Allusions*, by Indiana State University

Fates... Fates are not always held high.
The birds sing and the air is calm.
Nature sits all around me, leaving me chilled
With all sorts of emotions.

Although the clouds all sit above,
All there is would be peace.
Is this how the world will end?
Is this how my life will end?

The feelings I have are charged with my power.
Everything around me is out of my control,
So it'd be natural to only worry
About what I can grasp.

Love is not something I can grasp, but feel.
History stands against the type of love I feel.
In my heart, I know it's not possible and that
The feelings I have will never be expressed.

Never to be filled with laughter and pure happy emotion.
My love will go against nature and so too will my stance.
The time I spend will be lost to nothing but memory.
If I could just tell you how I feel...

The pain I feel does not match how the birds may chirp,
but the infatuation will never be returned.
Perhaps you'll just be happy with someone else,
And maybe our stories were never meant to collide.

My nerves are heavy from joy.
The day is ending and so too will these feelings.
Would that be the perfect world?
Are my fates settled? Are our fates settled?

If only you could know the truth.
My fate has to be sealed, and that much is true.
Though this fate could be revealed,
But you may never know.

"Not Dead Yet"

Originally published in the Student Literary Journal,
Allusions, by Indiana State University

There will be no one to hold my hand,
But I refuse to be like a dried fish in the sand.
The world around me is freezing over,
But I feel as lucky as a four-leaf clover.
I stand warmer than the sun and you cannot freeze me.

I stand firm and I holler,
But you may want me to wear a firm collar.
I will not bow down to control and instead I see
The crystal-clear world around me.

I will rise again like the dead,
And not meant to be filled with dread.
Although it might sound a bit cryptic,
It might also sound apocalyptic.
You forget, I am not dead yet.

My words might sound bland,
While I make a fist with my hand.
I do not trust you, and you do not trust me,
It might not help that you might be too blind to see.

I am not marked by a stone in the graveyard.
I am alive and well, holding up a card.
You do not have control over my life.
Once it is knocked out of your hand, I take the knife.
You forget that I am not dead just yet.

I will rise again like the dead,
And not meant to be filled with dread.
Although it might sound a bit cryptic,
It might also sound apocalyptic.
You forget, I am not dead yet.

No, I am not dead yet.
I will stand firm and I will continue to holler.
You might hate the way that I hold myself together,
But I will have a smile across my face.
No... I am not dead just yet.

You want me to whimper and cry,
I dealt the cards,
And that much is true.
But I do not lay in the ground yet.
I am alive and well and you may hate that.

I will rise again like the dead,
And not meant to be filled with dread.
Although it might sound a bit cryptic,
It might also sound apocalyptic.
You forget, I am not dead yet.

You're too late.
That poor and quiet little boy is too far gone now.
He faded away into the darkness,
You see, he got tired of you stepping all over him.
And what remains is not dead yet.

"He Who Gets Stuck in the Shallows"

Originally published in the Student Literary Journal, *Allusions*, by Indiana State University

He made his way through the high school gymnasium to find a seat. The homecoming basketball game was almost over, and he was rather nervous about the dance that was going to come up. As he got closer to the bleachers, a young girl stopped him in his tracks.

"Lloyd!" she cried. "It's great to see you here! I'm so happy that you're getting out of your shell!"

He sighed, "Yeah. I am."

Lloyd has always been a little bit more on the shyer side of things. He barely spoke out in school and was always afraid to talk to his classmates. This girl just happened to be the one exception.

After he passed the girl, he started talking to himself. "He wouldn't be late, would he? Why would he be late on our special night?" The game was almost over, and the dance would only be moments away. Lloyd was anxious, and he did not like the waiting game. He wouldn't leave him here all alone, would he? He promised.

Within a moment, another boy had tapped on Lloyd's shoulder. He looked to see who it was only for his face to immediately light up with joy. "Tazca! You're here!" Lloyd exclaimed, standing up to hug his lover.

"Of course, I am!" Tazca smiled. "Wouldn't want to miss our special day, would I?"

By now the game was over, and the principal stood in the center of the gymnasium to announce that the dance would be starting shortly. Lloyd's face grew a strong smile.

"Care to dance with me, babe?" Lloyd asked while his face blushed an intense red.

Tazca smiled, "Of course, I will!"

As they and many more people filed down to the dance floor after the music had started, Lloyd couldn't help but feel as if something was rather odd. He quietly dismissed these thoughts as Tazca began to lead him in a slow dance. Even though the pair danced and danced, something was still off, and Lloyd couldn't shake the feeling any longer. He had to bring up what was clouding his mind.

"We are going to tell the police about what we saw tomorrow, right?"

Tazca rolled his eyes, "Yes, babe, but let's focus on

our night for right now."

"How can I enjoy the night when I know something is wrong? We saw a man get murdered in the woods. He's got a family and I'm sure they are worried about him!"

"Lloyd, please. We are a gay couple in the middle of a time that most people want us crucified. We are lucky that no one is really paying attention to two guys dancing at this, and yet you want to spoil it."

"Tazca, please. You know that I can't stand by while someone is dead and that we could be helping catch the murderer!" Tazca laughed. "Why are you laughing, Tazca? This isn't funny!"

"But it is," Tazca joked. "You didn't even notice that your dad has gone missing?"

Lloyd froze, "What do you mean? My dad is in Hentonsville. We talked about this."

"He's not. The place that he's at is far away from here, and it's very warm," Tazca laughed. He grabbed Lloyd and pulled him close. "You'll see him soon. The entire town knows what you did."

"What do you mean what I did?" By now, Lloyd realized that the music had stopped and everyone was staring at him. "What is going on?" he questioned.

"He's the one we want," Tazca laughed while pointing. "He killed his dad and many others!"

"I-I what?" Lloyd asked as he looked all around the room. Everyone was getting closer and closer to him. "I didn't hurt anybody!"

"I'm sorry, Lloyd," said the girl from earlier. "We can't let you leave."

But what did he do? His fight-or-flight response had kicked in. Lloyd managed to escape everyone in the room, and he ran straight home.

"He's heading home! We have to stop him!" One had said.

Lloyd ran as fast as he could. Luckily, his house was a few blocks away from the school. He ran to the porch of his house and locked the door behind him. Not knowing what to do, he quickly barricaded the door with a coffee table and a dining room chair. He ran up the stairs and sat in his room. Tears had escaped his eyes, and they clouded his vision. He acted in a frenzy just to ensure that he had a fighting chance. No one would break into his home. No one could do anything to him here. He was safe... or at least so he thought.

"Set fire to the mansion!" a man yelled.

"Go to hell!" another person had cried.

"Suffer as they did!" a man screamed.

"DIE! DIE! DIE!" they all chanted.

Tazca was the one who lit the torch, and he smiled as he threw it at the door to the mansion. "Be it damned, I hereby curse you as a shadow in the shallows. You will walk the Earth as nothing but a spirit. Goodbye, the Shadow in the Shallows."

The fire had spread quickly to the entire house, taking away every piece of life. Lloyd could do nothing except retreat to a corner, where he wept. He did nothing to deserve this, but in his mind, he felt as if he deserved this. He felt as if God was punishing him, punishing him for being bisexual and punishing him for the fact that he fell in love. Death was the only option now. Lloyd had lived far too much, and he deserved what was coming.

The flames were upstairs now. Lloyd stayed still and he closed his eyes. "I am a shadow. I deserve this. I shouldn't have been able to live in the first place.

The heat was so much that Lloyd had to open his eyes, which only were burning from the smoke. He saw the red, fiery flames illuminate his room, showing the infinite doom that would capture him.

He closed his eyes again. "Dad, I'm so sorry that I'm not the son you wanted. Sis, I'm sorry that I wasn't ever there for you. I deserve this. I accept my fate."

The air began to feel cold as a white light captured the entire room. Lloyd began to wonder if he had died by this point and was sent to heaven... and so he opened his eyes, only to see that he was still in his room, which was now completely black and white, absent of color in its entirety. The flames, however, were still red, echoing the display of violence that the house had been put under. The strange thing was, those flames were no longer hot, and Lloyd didn't even feel them as they passed through him.

The fire department arrived, and they were able to extinguish all of the flames from the charred mansion. The people waited anxiously as the fire department was able to state that there was no one found inside. Did Lloyd escape? Did he die there and the firefighters just happened to make a mistake?

Lloyd froze in place, wondering what had happened, but a floating apparition appeared before he could process anything.

"This is your second chance," it said. "You are cursed to be a shadow person and so you are free to do as you see fit, except live with the land of the living."

"Did I perish in those flames?" he asked it.

The being shook its head, "You are an extraordinary being. You are neither living nor dead."

What could this mean for the shadow? "What shall I do now? Was I supposed to suffer an eternity of torture? Am I damned to nothingness for the remainder of the universe?"

"You tell me."

The shadow was speechless. He was stuck with so many questions, and before he could even ask any of them, the being had disappeared. The shadow sighed, pouting in his place. Days would pass before he could finally move. He wondered about the role of shadows in the world. They must be similar to ghosts, capable of haunting others, and so Lloyd was going to do just that. He was going to haunt the living. He finally brought himself to the front of his house, and he was bracing himself for the world he was about to open up to.

The sun was shining, and the world resumed just like normal. The porch to the mansion was broken down and charred as well, but Lloyd was able to step outside. He just needed to go further... he wanted to be out in that sun. So, he did just that. With every shallow step that he took, he was braving for what was coming. He was almost there, and he needed to take that last step.

His foot reached for the sunlight in its attempt to reach for a new beginning, but once it was out in the sunlight, it started to smell like burnt hair. Before Lloyd could even grasp what was happening, his foot had engulfed in flames. He recoiled, landing backward on the porch. He grasped his foot while he was wincing in pain.

Haunting was out of the question. He could not even escape the mansion, let alone haunt a person. Defeated, he stayed back in his mansion, and he lived there for the next fifty years.

Throughout this time, he had seen many events happen throughout history. He saw the end of the Vietnam War on a portable television that somehow survived the fire of the mansion. Lloyd wished that many of his old friends from school were able to return back to Cooperton, living their lives with their families. He also saw the resignation of President Nixon and wondered what this could mean for the country as a whole. He saw the rise of the HIV/AIDS crisis in the eighties, which caused a great deal of fear in the shadow.

By the time the nineties hit, the old portable television had become broken. This forced Lloyd to go to the neighboring houses at night, just to see what the television had on. Due to this, Lloyd was watching the news less and less, but he was able to see something that he had never expected in his new life. On the night of September 11, 2001, he walked to the neighbor's window only to see recapped footage of a plane hitting each of the towers of the World Trade Center, and both buildings falling to their demise. This had upset Lloyd, just as it had upset everyone else living in the nation. The tears that escaped Lloyd's eyes were blue, echoing the despair that he had felt.

The year was 2020, and Lloyd had been staying in the mansion for fifty years. The world was in a different place than it was fifty years ago. Lloyd had wondered about whether everyone's memory was trifled with by Tazca, for it had to be him that Lloyd was turned into this ghastly state in the first place. Unbeknownst to Lloyd, it was true. Everyone in Cooperton had forgotten about the fact that they were the ones who set the mansion on fire. They thought that an accident had started the flames that consumed the mansion. As for the murder, they were able to capture one of the boys responsible, but unfortunately, Lloyd had never found this out.

Now in 2020, still convinced that he deserved all

that had happened to him, he lived in the shallows that he was damned to. This would be his fate until the end of time, and there would be no one to convince him otherwise. That was until a cat showed up at the shadow's door.

Lloyd tried to drown out the cat's cries, but he eventually gave in. He opened the charred door to the mansion, only to find a black cat with green eyes sitting in front and center.

"What brings you here... here that is so far from hope?" The shadow asked.

The cat had meowed as if it was in a strange reply.

"Go back to where you once came. There is no hope or pride here, there is only desolation and devastation.

The cat meowed again.

"Do my words not plague you? I asked you to leave this place and never return!"

The cat had let out a long and drawn-out meow.

The shadow's eyes turned a fiery red, echoing the violence that had once been inflicted upon him. "Leave. Please. I asked you with the utmost politeness. I do not wish to be bothered, and those who happen to bother me end up in distress. Leave this place."

The cat meowed once again, with the shadow having a

long sigh. There was the sound of someone clearing their throat, leaving the shadow with one eyebrow being raised over the other.

"I've come to declare a decree... a decree from a failed knight that was once in a position similar to yours," the voice had said, mimicking the shadow.

"Who said that?" Lloyd had asked.

"Down here," the cat had said to Lloyd's reply.

"A talking cat? Am I that far gone from reality that my mind plays endless tricks upon me?"

"I am no talking cat," the cat laughed. "I am a familiar, and I am here to bring a message for you- the shadow in the shallows."

"I do not need a message. I just want to be left alone." The shadow sighed, looking away from the cat.

"Oh, but I assure you, shadow. You do need this message. You are a piece of a huge prophecy and don't panic just yet. You are one out of thousands."

"Prophecy?" the shadow inquired. "What kind of prophecy?"

The cat laughed, "Incoming doom and redemption-arc thing."

"Redemption-arc thing..." The shadow sighed, "Why

would I ever agree to this?"

The cat laughed once more, "Because it would mean that you would become a human again. You would be able to live a life, not of torture, but a life worth living. Doesn't that sound important?"

"I do not agree with such things," the shadow stated. "It is impossible."

"Nothing is impossible. Look at you. You are a shadow person. Tell me, if this was impossible, wouldn't you be impossible?"

That was a valid point. This simple statement made the shadow question everything that he had endured for the last fifty years. What was the point of Lloyd undergoing this trauma? What was the point of the cat's claims? What was the truth behind being stuck in the shadows? With all of this stuck in his mind, hanging on the edge of the cliff, Lloyd had decided to hear more of the cat's claims, and at the end of the day, the Shadow in the Shallows was in fact interested in hearing more.

For once in fifty years, the shadow had a glimpse of what was a brand-new beginning, and in the end, he would have to learn how to be human once again.

"Mythical Reborn"

Originally Written for *Death and the Groomsman*

In the beginning, the universe of Mythical was constructed in seventy-eight Earth weeks during what Earth Scientists call "The Big Bang." The one who created it was He-Who-Thrones-Thee and he was an overseer of the universes. When he angered the goddess, Kndra, for meddling with various universes, he created a universe that would support his own life force.

After the universe was constructed, He-Who-Thrones-Thee got to work on creating the materials necessary to construct planets and stars. Eventually, through this method, one of the main ones; being named "Earth," would be where many of our stories begin. He also sectioned off the universe so that each of his children would control a portion of it. His first child was Platrom and he made him the governor of the Heavens, the second child was Quanta, and the third child was Auburn. Quanta and Auburn would split the normal realm into two and they would govern a section each. However, both sisters failed to keep their relationship peaceful and a war was the result.

The fourth child was Theotorix, and he was the original governor of the mental realm. There were dozens of other children that He-Who-Thrones-Thee gave birth to and they too would rule various realms of the universe. However, the final child, Fatala would be the governor of the underdeveloped realms. Purgatory and Hell would be listed as such, but somehow, Fatala was never able to live in either of those realms.

Platrom was the only one who could use He-Who-Thrones-Thee's gift to birth children out of thought. This was how he created all of his angels, including the most notorious one of them, Lucifer. Due to Lucifer's countless acts of rebellion, he would be cast out of Heaven and left to be the governor of Hell.

Theotorix, Quanta, Auburn, and Fatala would live in harmony for most of their days until the birth of the war between Quanta and Auburn. Their father alone ruled the universe, but the siblings all grew restless before going their separate ways.

A few of these realms began to support life, which caused the need to have governors in the first place. For example, civilizations started to emerge on various planets in the universe, including "Earth." Purgatory started to do the same thing, with various species of organisms emerging. This therefore meant that the guardians of Mythical arose, something that He-Who-Thrones-Thee did not expect. For the Grim Reapers, their guardian was Acron. For the Shadow People, it was Skantrania. Although these were two out of the many guardians that once existed, they are the ones that we look up to when it comes to stories surrounding the Grim Reapers and the Shadow People. Acron was the original Grim Reaper, and he was the one who made his way to purgatory, freeing it from the treacherous Fatala. He founded the city of Grimstin and made it the capital of Purgatory.

Acron would note that the birth of new life would mean that organisms would ultimately end in death too and so he began recruiting all over the normal realm. The Grim Reapers would live in a country called Repatas and would be able to travel freely between the normal realm and Purgatory. Grimstin would therefore become the main base of operations.

The next issue was that He-Who-Thrones-Thee made the universe of Mythical in a way that would support his life force. No universe like this one was ever created before, and those who lived in the other universes were unable to hold any sort of special ability. In Mythical, supernatural entities began to emerge, and there was no limit on what could exist.

The normal realm is plagued with vampires, ghouls, the undead, demons, monsters, ghosts, shadows, and so much more. There is no way to stop the madness. Surprisingly, Mythical has lasted this long, let alone the fact that the reality of this universe remains in a fixed place. The best way to ensure peace and order is by having each civilization remain unaware of the truth of the universe. Individuals are always bound to find out, but the guardians have always watched over every single supernatural being as well as every mortal being in the universe to ensure the safety of the greater good. They gather in secret in a place that is completely lost of knowledge of all beings and records say that they can never agree on anything.

He-Who-Thrones-Thee also did not foresee that due to the nature of this universe's composition, it, in fact, created a sentient being within itself. The universe was capable of its own thought and began to seek its freedom from its tyrannical leader. Seeing that its father had been enslaving all sorts of beings across the universe, it forged its own creation from a science experiment on Earth in the year 1969. This experiment turned into a "human" fetus with various gifts granted by the universe to stop anyone who would become a follower of He-Who-Thrones-Thee, which were coined as The Followers of the Branchless Tree, seeking to return the universe to its natural state and enslaving all creatures in the name of what they call "The Serpent." In all truth, The Serpent was just another name for He-Who-Thrones-Thee but was labeled in this manner due to the being's serpent-like shape while enslaving the universe.

The experiment was named the Nintarius Olfroxicus (also known as the Nintus Olfrox), and he was charged with finding various individuals who might be a key to defeating The Branchless. He alone is the leader of the rebellion against The Serpent and his followers.

Except, Nintus Olfrox has never been up against the Serpent himself. The Serpent was already imprisoned by a rising hero before Nintus' birth. Now that the hard part was already done, this just meant that Nintus and his friends had to ensure that no Branchless member was able to revive their lost leader. Whether or not he succeeds, will be hard to tell.

So, dear readers, this is where our stories shall begin. Mythical is a world of strange possibilities and problems, and you shall see what happens firsthand.

"I Feel My Pulse"

I feel my pulse.
My head is killing me.
I think I acted on impulse.
My body is divided into three.

I get out of bed,
I brush my hair and teeth.
I feel so dead,
My blood drips beneath.

Today's the day,
I get to appear strong.
I'll rule the day today,
Acting like nothing's wrong.

It's a good thing that I'm a poet,
And not a deranged serial killer.
I'm in pain, but I can't show it.
My life's such a thriller.

Everyday is like this,
I get to act like nothing's wrong,
But the truth is, my heart did miss.
I have to stay strong.

I go to work,
I do my job,
My doubts lurk,
I'm chased by an angry mob.

I get home,
I wish I lived in a rom-com,
My thoughts get to roam,
My words died in my palm.

Every day I get questioned,
"What's next in your plans?"
Wishing I could go unquestioned
As I try to figure out my plans.

They're all nosey, always probing,
When all I wanna do is die.
The lights might as well be strobing.
Let me go cry,

DAMN IT!

I should be nicer,
Try to be kinder,
Even though my rights are in a slicer.
My work stuck in a binder.

I feel my pulse,
My head is killing me.
I just want people to leave me be,
Not wanting to act on impulse.

This is my problem, isn't it?
I'm always focusing on just me.
While the world buried me in a pit
From which I can't see.

It's getting harder to breathe,
I've fallen out of a tree.
I'm starting to seethe,
People are toying with me.

All I want is to be left alone,
Figuring out what I want.
To mock, but atone
By the ghosts that haunt.

I feel my pulse.
My heart is beating.
I haven't acted on impulse,
I haven't been cheating.

My fates aren't unknown,
For I'm not dead yet.
My work's not been thrown,
I haven't made a bet yet.

It's not over yet.
I'm not a ghost writer.
Even in a looming threat,
My future's getting brighter.

Dear Memories,
We had a good run,
With our great accessories,
We're gonna have fun.

All this time,
I've been where I am.
I'm still in my prime.
I refuse to give a damn.

I'm not stuck in the shallows,
I live before you.
I didn't die at the gallows.
We get to see this through.

I'm not *The Shadow in the Shallows.*
I'm stronger than *Death and the Groomsman,*
Stronger than any sort of gallows,
I feel like an accomplished newsman.

I crossed *The Bridge Filled With Marigolds,*
My power is wrapped around my skin.
This is all worth more than all the golds.
Warm up the car, we're going for a spin!

Even though I lost him,
I still have to thrive.
I might look grim,
But we all made it out alive.

The Hollowed Dreams
Were conquered.

F. L. Day is ***NOT***
Anguished to the Grave
He made it out
        ALIVE.

"It's a Wonderful Day to be Alive"

It's a wonderful day to be alive.
I just saved my future to my hard drive.
I feel so accomplished today,
I might actually get my way.

I'm so tired of feeling like a waste.
I write my words out with great haste.
Is it bad that I have to
See myself through?

Stop trying to drag me down,
You're only looking like a clown.
I know my self-worth,
I have a place on this earth.

I'm tired of being the bad guy,
I'm tired of being seen as a mad man.
I'm tired of being apathetic,
For I'm only just me.
Someday, I'll be free.

Goodbye Darkness, Goodbye Depression.
You almost caused my regression.
My successes send me to cloud nine,
Where I'll finally be fine.

It's a wonderful day to be alive,
I see a future where I can thrive.
I'll pick myself up from the ground,
With my reasons to live, which I've found.

Acknowledgements

Where exactly do I begin? Thank you to everyone who has cheered me on for creating this book. Thank you to everyone who has been there for me while I've been charting through my writing journey for the past several years. Thank you to everyone who purchased and/or read this book. Thank you to everyone who I have met throughout the creation of this book and in the midst of marketing it on social media.

That all sounds really lame, but in truth, the creation of this book was only possible because I've gained my voice, something that was only possible due to the various people in my life who have been there for me. That being said, I have to give a huge thank you to my PRR-Team, filled with my fantastic coworkers who have been cheering me on and have watched me grow firsthand. Among this team, I have to say thank you to Debbie who has cheered me on and has shown me endless support since the very beginning! Thank you to Gabe who has told me that I am one of the most successful people that he knows and has always been there for me through the good, the bad, and the ugly. Thank you to Charlotte, who has given me fantastic advice and has been there for my endless rantings about the book and about my life. Thank you to all my other PRR-Team Members who have also cheered me and have been watching me do the thing... AGAIN!

Special thanks to the Indiana State University Writing Center Team as well! I have so many wonderful (former) coworkers that I still am connected to and still value their feedback and help even after graduating college! Thank you to Robin who has watched me continue my writing and professional journeys and has also cheered me on!

Thank you to the Creative Writing Society, filled with wonderful friends who have been there with their support every time that I give them an update about my works and updates about me. I have missed the community that we've had! Special thanks to Carrie who helped me with the book cover and gave me valuable feedback! Thank you again to Alice who helped with the beginning of *Death and the Groomsman*, who also supported my decision to re-purpose the lore-dumping scene (even though she had no idea that I was inserting it into *Anguished to the Grave*). Thank you to Destiny who looked at some of my poems and gave me really good feedback!

Thank you to the Alpha Delta Phi Society's New Leaf Chapter for not only being fantastic siblings, but for also cheering me on with the creation of both *The Hollowed Dreams* and *Anguished to the Grave*. Your support has never gone unnoticed, and I can't thank you all enough!

Thank you to the History Club, filled with friends who have also cheered me on in the past, and to Lauren for being an amazing friend!

Thank you to all of my friends from Indiana State University who have watched me make two books in the span of one year. Keep being amazing and I can't wait for you all to see what comes next!

Big thank you to Emma Ellis. She has been an amazing friend and is an amazing author. I can't recommend her works enough! She helped me so much with my various questions through the self-publishing process and I couldn't have accomplished any of this if it wasn't for her! Check out her books, *Wicked Cruel Things*, *All the Violent Ways*, and *Deadly Vicious Lies*!

Finally, thank you to my friends and family who have watched me create this book, especially my mother who has listened to my problems with this book. I can't thank her enough. Above all, I love you all, whether you're a reader, a friend, a family member, or a coworker! This was possible because of you all! Remember that the world is a better place because you exist in it! Keep being wonderful and amazing! Never give up on your dreams!